So You Want to be the Perfect Family?

We were a perfectly ordinary family until a few months ago. It was then that we set out on an unusual adventure We didn't move to a remote island in the Outer ides or a hillside farm in the Pyrenees. We didn't go any where. No, we stayed at home and everything happened here.

n Katie answers an advertisement to take part in a television make-over programme, she doesn't realize what is getting into. Because what is going to be made over er family—to turn it into a Perfect Family, where ything runs smoothly and nobody argues; where the se is always tidy and meals are cooked properly and on . But when your family is as chaotic as Katie's, is that g to be possible? Do they really want to be perfect? they cope with the instant fame that comes with being levision? And what will all her friends think about it?

HINE FEENEY was born in Leicester in 1956 and has seven rs and sisters. Her parents both come from the west of Ireland. iving school she trained to be a special needs teacher. She had writing since she was at school, and while teaching in Yorkshire ended a writers' group and started to write seriously. In 1987 she o Essex and had her first radio play accepted by the BBC. She ved back to Leicester to take up writing full time and had her published in 1994. She is married, with two children, and re time she enjoys listening to music, playing her accordion, going on picnics *So You Want to be the Perfect Family?* is her first b

So You Want to be the Perfect Family?

OTHER OXFORD BOOKS

SO YOU WANT TO BE
THE PERFECT FAMILY?

Josephine Feeney

Illustrated by Rachel Merriman

OXFORD
UNIVERSITY PRESS

OXFORD
UNIVERSITY PRESS

Great Clarendon Street, Oxford OX2 6DP
Oxford University Press is a department of the University of Oxford.
It furthers the University's objective of excellence in research, scholarship,
and education by publishing worldwide in

Oxford New York

Auckland Bangkok Buenos Aires
Cape Town Chennai Dar es Salaam Delhi Hong Kong Istanbul
Karachi Kolkata Kuala Lumpur Madrid Melbourne Mexico City Mumbai
Nairobi São Paulo Shanghai Singapore Taipei Tokyo Toronto

With an associated company in Berlin

British Library Cataloguing in Publication Data available

ISBN 0 19 275233 2

3 5 7 9 10 8 6 4

Designed and typeset by Mike Brain Graphic Design Limited, Oxford
Printed in Great Britain by
Cox & Wyman Ltd, Reading, Berkshire

For my daughter,
Faffa McKay,
who would love to have the perfect family.

Would you like to live in a perfect family? Would you like a life where everything runs smoothly and nothing ever goes wrong? We did. We wanted to be a perfect family. And it made us famous. Really, really famous. People stopped us on the street and turned us around and said, 'Yes, it's them!'

Everybody thinks that it's brilliant being famous and some people say that's all they want to be when they grow up.

But we didn't set out to be famous, we just wanted to turn our family into a better one. If your life's not perfect and you want to make your family a better one, read my story. You might think again.

Part One

Meet The Family

Meet The Family

Meet my family—the Rossi family. We're perfectly ordinary. Not perfect, by any means. We're not outstanding either. If you saw us shopping in the town centre you wouldn't stop and say, 'Wow, look at that family!' You probably wouldn't even notice us.

My dad is Michael Rossi. He's the grandson of Luigi Rossi who set up an ice cream empire in Birmingham in the 1930s, so Dad's always telling us. Unfortunately for Dad, the empire melted and there were no great Rossi millions to inherit, so my dad had to find his own fortune. At the moment he works as a storyteller; actually a storyteller-in-residence at Felixton Hall.

My mum, Annie Rossi, is a student and she works part-time in a pork pie factory. There are two children in our family, Ronan and me, Katie. Mum will tell you that we're lovely children and she's very proud of us but she's bound to say that, isn't she? She's our mother. At home, Mum doesn't say that; she says things like, 'Can't you stop arguing?' and 'Who's going to tidy this mess up?' and 'What did I do to deserve this?' and 'Tell them, Michael!' You see, me and Ronan are perfectly ordinary children. We fight and argue like everybody else. We're not perfect.

I would love to be perfect. I try very, very hard, especially at school. 'She's a great trier,' my teachers say.

My mum and dad smile and say, 'She may be a great trier at school but at home she's very trying!' At present, I am trying to encourage hedgehogs to make their home in the garden which isn't an easy thing to do. I want to have my own pet hedgehog because Mum and Dad won't let me have a cat or a rabbit or a guinea pig. It seems as though a hedgehog is the next best thing.

Ronan, my older brother, thinks I'm daft trying to encourage hedgehogs into the garden. Ronan is far from being perfect. He's going through that difficult age where mums and dads and little sisters are merely annoying details about life. (Well, that's what Mum says.) He thinks his family is far from perfect but he knows there's very little that he can do about it. Most of his energies are channelled into his running because, one day, he wants to be a world-class runner.

So, that's us—the Rossi family. A perfectly ordinary family. That is, we were a perfectly ordinary family until a few months ago. It was then that we set out on an unusual adventure. We didn't sell our house and buy an ocean-going yacht so we could sail around the world. We didn't move to a remote island in the Outer Hebrides or a hillside farm in the Pyrenees. We didn't go anywhere.

No, we stayed at home and everything happened here.

The Advertisement

It all started one morning in February with an innocent advertisement tucked away on the inside pages of the paper. Me and Dad loved reading those quirky little adverts. Sometimes they said things like: *'Did you have an unhappy childhood? Daytona at Channel 4 would like to talk to you about it . . .'* But on this cold, February morning, this is what the advertisement said:

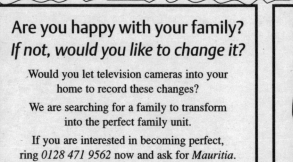

Are you happy with your family?
If not, would you like to change it?

Would you let television cameras into your home to record these changes?

We are searching for a family to transform into the perfect family unit.

If you are interested in becoming perfect, ring *0128 471 9562* now and ask for *Mauritia*.

Give us a call—we're waiting to hear from you.

'They'll probably get millions of enquiries about that,' Dad said, pointing at the advert and smiling broadly.

'What, Dad?' I asked, in between mouthfuls of Super Caramettes.

'This,' Dad pointed again, whilst taking several boxes of cereal out of the larder cupboard. He shook an empty cereal box.

Ronan rushed into the kitchen, his shirt and tie flapping in the breeze that he was creating. 'Dad?' he called.

'What's up with you?' Dad asked, leaning against the sink warming his hands around his huge coffee mug.

'Everything! Mum's hogging the bathroom, my hair's sticking up, I've got no hair gel left, my kit hasn't been washed, I've got a training session at eight and I bet there's no cereal left for me,' Ronan complained.

I carried on eating in silence because I knew what was going to happen next. I didn't look at Ronan, I stared at the advert about making the perfect family and tried to imagine how wonderful it would be if we were perfect. I would just love my family to be perfect, I thought. I would love us to be on the telly.

'You rotten pig, Katie!' Ronan shouted. 'You've eaten all the Super Caramettes.'

'There were hardly any left anyway,' I replied, calmly. 'And Dad said we have to finish off these boxes before he buys any more and don't call me a pig just because *you* don't get up on time.'

'I've got nothing to eat for breakfast and I've got a training session . . .'

'At eight, yes, we know, Ronan. Look, there are six boxes of cereal here,' Dad pleaded. 'Surely there must be something . . .'

'And I don't like any of them,' Ronan said as he shook each box aggressively.

'The early bird catches the worm,' I said, before Ronan tried to snatch my precious bowl away. 'You should get up earlier.'

'Shut up, Katie!' Ronan snapped. 'You and your stupid sayings.'

'Ronan,' Dad interrupted. 'That's enough of that.' He fired a warning glance at Ronan.

'There aren't even any rotten cornflakes!' Ronan complained.

'That's because I always throw away any rotten cornflakes,' Dad said, leaning against the sink and looking over my shoulder at the paper.

'Very funny—der!' Ronan said whilst glancing at his reflection in the oven door and knotting his school tie. 'I'll just have to buy some chocolate and crisps on the way to school.'

As he was talking, Mum bustled into the kitchen, flustered and rushed. She was always like this when she had an early start at the factory.

'There's no cereal, Mum,' Ronan pleaded.

'There are about ten boxes of cereal in that cupboard. Choose something and eat it,' Mum said, firmly, without standing still. 'Mike, can you run me up the Leys? I'm on at eight this morning.' Dad immediately started clearing the table and washing up. Then he started sorting out breakfast for Mum.

'What about *me*?' Ronan asked, holding out both hands as if pleading for mercy.

'What *about* you?' Mum and Dad chorused together.

'I thought Dad was going to run *me* to school. I've got a training session at eight,' Ronan said, stuffing his hands into his trouser pockets, trying to look like a deprived orphan. He does this very often.

'What's wrong with your bike?' Mum asked as she poured boiling water into a mug.

'It's punctured,' Ronan said, flatly. He stood in the middle of the kitchen, looking a bit punctured himself. Mum and Dad were both rushing about and he was just standing there, making the kitchen look untidy.

'What about Katie's bike?' Mum stirred the hot tea.

'He's not riding my bike!' I shouted. The cheek of it! Mum didn't even ask me.

'I'm not riding a *pink* bike!' Ronan protested.

'Look, Ronan,' Mum said as she moved Ronan towards a chair with her hands firmly on his shoulders. 'You are going to sit down here and have the cereal I give you. Then you are going to walk quickly to school for your training session.'

'Your toast Annie,' Dad said, placing some hot toast and jam on the table. 'Sit down for a minute and eat it.'

'I haven't got time. I need to pack my stuff for my class this afternoon,' Mum said. 'Come on, Ronan, eat up!'

'Grape, prune, coconut, and fig flakes?' Ronan squirmed. 'Do I have to?'

'Yes!' Mum snapped, in between mouthfuls of toast and tea. 'Mike, you'll have to sort out this cereal business. We seem to have arguments about cereal every day. It's getting ridiculous.'

'Me?' Dad asked, surprised. 'They won't eat it.'

'Don't buy any more until they've eaten all that,' Mum

said. 'I'll have to finish my toast in the car,' Mum bustled about the kitchen, balancing her toast in her mouth.

'Oh, I wish you wouldn't finish your toast in the car, love. There's half a loaf of mouldy, unfinished toast underneath the front seat,' Dad complained as he searched under plates and newspapers for the car keys.

'I'm not *allowed* to take food into the factory—health and safety regulations . . .' Mum mumbled as she chewed her toast.

'Why don't we give all *this* to the Oxfam shop?' Ronan suggested as he stared disdainfully at his cereal.

'Because . . .' Mum began but then she glanced at the clock. 'Mike, come on. I'll be docked pay if I'm late.' Mum dashed about the kitchen gathering her overall, hat, and books together with one hand and carrying her hot mug of tea with the other. 'Do you want me to bring any pork pies home for you?' she asked.

'No!' Ronan shouted.

'What about my sandwiches?' I asked.

'I'll be back in time to make them,' Dad replied quickly.

'What about my *training*?' Ronan bellowed.

'Walk!' Mum replied, half out of the door.

'I'll be too tired for my training . . .' Ronan complained, following Mum and Dad to the front door.

'It'll do you good,' Mum called. Then she rushed back and kissed us both. Ronan made a great show of wiping away the kiss because he thinks that's what fourteen-year-old boys are supposed to do. 'Love you!' Mum shouted before she disappeared.

'What about this advert, Dad?' I reminded him.

'We'll sort it out later,' Dad said. 'Oh, Annie, you're not

12

taking your tea in the car again. Half of our mugs are in the car . . .'

'Well, bring them in when you get home,' Mum shouted, before slamming the car door. 'Come on, I'll be late.'

I watched Dad's car move quickly away from the kerb. Back in the kitchen, Ronan was emptying his cereal into the bin and muttering about our wonderful parents.

'Brilliant—no breakfast and I've got to walk to training,' he muttered. 'I'll probably faint.'

'Stop moaning, Ronan,' I replied.

'It's pathetic! I *hate* my family,' Ronan said, throwing himself on to the sofa in the lounge.

'No, you don't,' I corrected him. I cleared the rest of the dishes from the table and left them in a pile for Dad to wash.

'Well . . . I hate them in the morning,' Ronan conceded.

'I think I know how we can make things better,' I suggested as I wiped the kitchen table.

'How?' Ronan asked, as if it was a total impossibility.

'Wait and see,' I said. 'Aren't you going to training?'

I had already decided that as soon as Ronan left for training, I would ring that number and speak to Mauritia.

And I did. She wasn't there so I left a clear message on her answer machine.

The Letter

The letter from the television company arrived one Saturday morning. It was addressed to me because I had made the phone call. I was quite excited because I didn't get many letters.

Mum was asleep in bed after a late shift at the pork pie factory; Dad was sitting at the table with his feet up on another chair reading the Saturday paper. Ronan was sprawled across the settee in the living room, watching the chart countdown on television. (Ronan is supposed to be very fit but most of the time he's extremely lazy.)

Dad was curious as soon as he saw the letter. 'What's this, Katie? Have you been writing to someone at Heartlands Television?'

I smiled and shrugged my shoulders. 'Sort of,' I said.

'You little tinker,' he said brightly. 'What've you been up to?'

I opened the letter. It was from Mauritia, about *Perfect Families*. I scanned it quickly and then passed it to Dad. 'You'll have to fill it in,' I said.

'Did you ring up then?' Dad asked.

'Yes.'

'I was going to but I never got around to it,' Dad said, absentmindedly, as he turned the information over and over.

'Anyone made any toast yet?' Ronan yelled. 'I'm starving.'

'Make it yourself, Ronan,' I called. At times his laziness really got to me.

'Keep your voices down, kids. I want your mum to have a bit of a lie-in this morning,' Dad said.

'Why, is she poorly?' Ronan enquired as he slithered around the kitchen in his pyjamas and thick, white socks. He looked pathetic.

'No she's very tired—it's really hard work in that factory, you know,' Dad said.

Ronan searched noisily in the bread bin. 'Where's the bread?' he asked, desperately.

'Try the freezer,' Dad suggested, without looking up from the letter.

'Oh no! It'll be frozen,' Ronan moaned. He pulled open the door of the freezer. 'Yuck—there's only brown bread in here.'

I giggled at the sight of Ronan in his pyjamas staring into the half empty freezer. 'You're such a moaner, Ronan,' I said.

Ronan glared at me menacingly. 'You know I hate brown bread, Dad,' he said.

'Sorry, Ronan—that's all we have,' Dad said, absorbed with the letter from Mauritia. 'It'll taste better once it's toasted.'

Ronan snatched the bread from the freezer and plonked it on to the breadboard. He sawed away at one end of it. 'This is totally frozen,' he complained.

Mum shuffled into the kitchen and glared at Ronan.

'What?' Ronan asked, in response to Mum's stare.

'Ronan, can't you keep your voice down for once on a Saturday morning? I was trying to sleep,' Mum said, in between yawns.

'It's not my fault, I was only . . .' Ronan began.

Mum yawned again and waved her hand at Ronan. 'I just want a little bit of peace on Saturday morning.'

'Still tired?' Dad asked, lifting his feet off the chair.

'Yes,' Mum sighed, dropping into the chair Dad's feet had vacated. 'The minute I drop off, I see pork pies moving across my brain on a conveyor belt and then I start getting anxious about taking them off the belt on time and putting them into the tray.'

'Weird,' Ronan said, as he stood with the frozen brown loaf in one hand and the bread knife in another.

'It's not weird if it's actually happening to you, Ronan,' I said. Ronan stuck his tongue out at me in response.

'Then I had a different dream about doing my revision in the middle of the factory and one of the girls took my notes away from me and she started using them to wrap pork pies,' Mum continued.

I sat at the far end of the table, reading the information from Heartlands Television. 'This'll cheer you up, Mum,' I said. 'Take your mind off pork pies.'

'More than a cup of tea would, hint, hint?' Mum suggested.

'Sorry, love,' Dad said, levering himself from his chair. 'I'll put the kettle on.'

'Katie, you're not scratching your head again are you?' Mum asked as she read through the letter.

'A bit,' I admitted. I'd been scratching it quite a lot but I didn't like to let on because I hated the treatment for nits. I absolutely *detested* the smell of the tea-tree conditioner that Mum dragged through my hair with a nit comb.

'We'll have to sort it out after breakfast,' Mum said as she poured milk into her tea. 'Ronan, make us a slice of toast, will you?'

Ronan was still battling with the frozen loaf. 'Need an axe for this,' he muttered.

'We should have taken it out yesterday,' Mum said, sipping her tea and wearily drawing back her hair from her face. 'Mind you, I was working late.'

'My fault,' Dad admitted, gently beating his fist against his chest.

'Nothing's ever right, is it?' Ronan asked, his face angrily screwed up in annoyance.

Mum sighed. 'I know it's a bit hard going at the moment but it'll soon be better, love, when my exams are over.'

'The bread's always frozen when you need it,' Ronan continued. 'There's never any of *my* favourite cereal, the toaster's broken so I always have to use our ancient grill, and I can never just enjoy my Saturday morning programmes!'

'What a hard life you lead, Ronan,' Mum said, exercising the muscles in her shoulder.

'D'you want to read my letter, Mum?' I said, trying to change the subject from Ronan's moaning.

'Anything interesting?' Mum asked.

'It's about this perfect family thing,' Dad said. 'Sounds like a great idea, sort of house and garden improvement job on the family.'

'Can we go for it?' I asked.

'Oh, we'll have to think about it, Katie. Is that toast made yet, Ronan?' Mum enquired. 'I'm starving.'

'I'm still trying to . . . cut it,' Ronan said sawing away at the frozen loaf. 'Why haven't we got a microwave like most normal families?'

'We have got one,' Mum replied.

'One that *works*,' Ronan added

'Can we go for it?' I asked again.

'Why don't we ever get anything fixed in this house?' Ronan questioned.

'Go for what, love?' Mum's mind was all over the place.

'Go for this perfect family thing,' I said.

'We don't need to,' Mum said, smiling. 'We're already perfect, aren't we?'

'You have *got* to be joking,' Ronan said, still sawing away at the loaf. Mum and Dad laughed; Ronan was never satisfied.

'Shall we go and have breakfast at the supermarket?' Mum suggested.

'What?' Ronan barked. 'After all the time it's taken me to cut one slice of bread.'

'It'll keep, Ronan,' Mum said, in between yawns. 'Give me five minutes to get ready.'

'She means twenty-five,' Ronan said.

'Come on, Ronan. You get yourself dressed too,' Dad suggested. 'Let's go soon, before they run out of bacon.'

The Decision

I was still thinking about our Saturday breakfast when I arrived at school on Monday morning. Every Monday, we have this thing called WOYS—it stands for Weekend Out Of Your System. We have twenty minutes at the beginning of the day when we're divided into groups of four and we talk about the weekend. Then when it's out of our system, we can really get down to work.

The Monday after we had bacon and eggs in Safeways, I told Isla, Krishna, and Conor about our breakfast.

'Well anyway, we went out for Sunday lunch,' Isla said, as if it was a competition.

'We went to a brilliant engagement party in Birmingham,' Krishna said, brightly.

'And guess what else . . .' I began, desperate to tell someone about our decision.

'Hey! It's my turn to say something,' Conor interrupted, shuffling on his chair. 'You've all had your go.'

'What did you do, Conor?' I asked in a laboured way because I wasn't interested in what Conor had to say.

'I went to me dad's and played football in the park with me mates,' Conor said.

'You say that every week,' Krishna complained.

'Well, that's what we do every week,' Conor said. 'Anyway, you're always going to weddings or parties.'

'No I'm not,' Krishna snapped. 'Sometimes we just go shopping.'

'Listen to this,' I began. 'We're going to be on the telly!'

'You? Why?' Isla asked.

'Well . . . we *might* be on the telly,' I conceded. 'We've applied for this thing about perfect families. It's like a make-over programme for a family.'

'That sounds brilliant,' Krishna said, excitedly.

'I know, I can't wait,' I said.

'My mum says anyone can get on the telly nowadays,' Conor said.

'Well, if Katie can get on, anyone can,' Isla agreed. 'Anyway . . .'

'There's no need to be like that, Isla,' I interrupted.

'Well, there's nothing special about your family,' Isla said. Sometimes I wonder why I'm friends with Isla. (I know it's mainly because we live close to one another and Isla's mum likes her to walk to school with me.) She can be really cutting and nasty at times but even I wasn't prepared for what came next. 'Your family's always doing things you can't afford,' Isla stated.

'Like what?' I asked, annoyed.

'Like going out for breakfast at Safeways,' Isla said.

Krishna giggled and shuffled in her chair. 'That's not expensive, Isla.'

'Yes it is,' Isla insisted. 'My mum says you don't spend money on the proper things.'

'Like what?' I asked again.

'Like . . . like . . . well, my mum says that the front of your house has needed painting for about three years and you never do anything about it.'

Then I laughed. That was so ridiculous. 'You're mad, Isla,' I said. 'It doesn't matter what the outside of your house looks like!'

'Yes it does!' Isla snapped. 'Houses like yours lower the tone of the neighbourhood. That's what my mum says.'

I laughed at that because Krishna was laughing, too, but inside I felt a bit empty. I was glad when Miss clapped her hands and asked us all to face the front. 'Right, that's the weekend out of your system. Now let's get down to business.'

I tried really hard to concentrate on literacy; we were doing about William Blake, but it was so hard. At first I kept thinking about what Isla said but then I sort of shook the top part of my body, quickly, as if to offload Isla's criticisms. Dad taught Ronan to do that because people can be really nasty to him after a race if he doesn't run as fast as they think he can.

Then I started thinking about Saturday, in Safeways. Talking about the *Perfect Families* thing. I was the most enthusiastic and Dad was very keen, too. 'I might get spotted, you never know,' Dad enthused. 'Someone might see that I'm an excellent storyteller and give me my own series on television.'

'I love those sort of programmes where you can see how people's homes and gardens are improved. I like watching their faces when . . .' I said.

'Somebody might spot my talent for running and I could get some kind of scholarship,' Ronan interrupted.

'What about you, Annie?' Dad asked.

Mum moved a piece of fried bread around with her fork. She seemed to be drawing a picture with the runny egg yolk.

'Annie?' Dad asked again.

'Honestly?' Mum said, looking up from her plate.

'Yes—tell us what *you* think,' Dad said. He leaned across the table as if he might draw the thoughts from her head.

'I don't like the idea at all,' Mum announced, moving her chair back.

'Why?' I asked. I was really disappointed that Mum felt like this.

'Keep your voice down, Katie,' Dad said, lifting his hand from the table as if calming things.

Mum leaned her head on her hand and sort of looked at us all sideways. 'I am only *just* coping . . . I think anything else would be too much.'

'It wouldn't,' I pleaded. 'It would be brilliant.'

'Katie, life isn't that straightforward. I've got an awful lot on my plate at the moment—my A levels, work, *and* you and Ronan,' Mum confided to us. 'And the house and the garden and . . .'

I folded my arms and slumped down in my chair. Typical! One of my parents always manages to put a dampener on things.

'Look, this is what I think we should do,' Dad suggested, placing his hands flatly on the table. 'Let's apply for it. Fill in the form and everything and if we don't get any further, fine. Nothing ventured . . .'

'Nothing gained,' I finished. Ronan looked up at the ceiling.

'What if we do get further?' Mum questioned.

'We could talk about it then but it's best not to rule ourselves out at this stage,' Dad reasoned.

The café was filling up and people were hovering about with full trays glaring at us, trying to move us with their stares. 'Let's go,' Mum said.

So after all that talking about it, we hadn't got very far. Me, Dad, and Ronan were very keen about *Perfect Families* but Mum wasn't.

I don't know why I said anything to Isla, Krishna, and Conor. And if more people were going to be like Isla—all negative and jealous—did I really want to be on the telly at all?

The Application

I thought about it all day at school and I wondered when Dad was going to post the application. It was still sitting on the workbench in the kitchen when I arrived home that evening. Dad hadn't sent it off. I took all the sheets out of the envelope and counted them—four. Mum must have written hers during the day, before she started her afternoon shift at the factory.

I tossed my schoolbag into the corner of the kitchen and slumped down on to the sofa in the lounge. I lay with my feet hanging over the far end and read what each of us had written for Mauritia, the producer of *Perfect Families*.

My Family by Ronan Rossi

In our family there's me, my sister Katie, and my mum and dad. I'll start with my dad—he is a full time storyteller and he gets a grant from the Midlands Area Lottery Team, MALT for short. Dad is absolutely brilliant at telling stories and I love it when our English teacher tells me I take after my dad. MALT has funded my dad for two years but they want a new storyteller from June so he has to get a different job. A lot of people don't understand about storytellers. Some of the lads at school, even some of my mates, say, 'Why doesn't your dad work?' and they say things like, 'Is your dad on the social?' I hate it when people say things like that, because storytelling is a proper job.

Mum works part-time at the moment because she's doing her A levels. She used to help out at a primary school, teaching children to read and write. Then one day she said, I think I could be a good teacher myself. That's when she decided to do her GCSEs and her A levels which she couldn't be bothered to do first time round because she was too busy enjoying herself at school—which you're not meant to do. At times it is very hectic in our house because my mum is always rushing off to work or to college and Dad looks

after the cooking and cleaning but sometimes
he forgets to do both.

I am fourteen and county champion in my age
group at Cross Country Running. I am absolutely
brilliant but I'm a bit of a fanatic too, like my
mum is about studying. In my school work I am
just about average at everything, apart from
telling stories but that doesn't count because it's
not really English. I train before school, three
times a week, and sometimes I train in the
evening, too.

I hope that someone high up in British athletics
notices me so that I can get sponsorship when I
leave school. I have always wanted to be brilliant
at running. My dad started taking me to a
running club because I had too much energy and I
used to drive him up the wall.

I think it would be really good to be on
television. Everyone could see how superb I am at
running. I think it would be good for our family,
too. I think we need some help to get us
organized—to make sure there's cereal I like for
breakfast and a toaster that actually works.

Why I want to be on the television
by Katie Rossi

I think it would be just brilliant to be on the telly. We could be on a programme like that one where people do up one another's houses.

I hope that Maisie Maykit from Decorating Delights will bring her sewing machine and do up my bedroom. I've got a really, really original idea for a new cover on my bed that makes it look like real hedgehogs, not prickly but sort of furry, if you know what I mean.

We are always having to make do in our house and this gets on my nerves a bit at times. Like when I needed new trainers, Mum said, 'You'll just have to make do for the time being,' and after a while I almost forgot about getting the new trainers because I was fed up with asking for them, even though my old trainers were hurting.

Mum and Dad always seem to be worried about money. Mum got a part-time job a few months ago to help make ends meet, whatever that means. One of my friends, Isla, says she feels sorry for me because my mum works in a factory. Her dad is a double-glazing manager and her mum is too busy in the house to have a job.

We need some help with our garden, too. I'm trying to get hedgehogs into our garden so that I can look after them. It would be brilliant if someone from the television could help me to build a small hut in our garden for the hedgehogs to use as a little house. I like being at the bottom of the garden, searching for hedgehogs and other wildlife. It's quiet and peaceful and there's no one arguing about who forgot to take the dinner out of the freezer for today's meal.

I think we would be a good family for this programme because we've got lots of ideas for things even though we sometimes forget to do anything with our ideas. We are not a perfect family. I would like us to be perfect, if not, a bit more normal than we are now.

Michael Rossi

First of all, I must say that this is an excellent idea. As a storyteller, I know that the very best stories in life are the real tales of everyday living. Quite often, we don't see our stories happening because we're characters in them.

That's why I would love to step outside our family, watch what is happening, and see how I can make things better; how we can all improve things. I know my wife, Annie, is not all that happy about applying but I'm sure a persuasive researcher or producer could help her to see how good it could be.

As I said, I work as a storyteller. I'm a freelance worker, but at the moment I'm at Felixton Hall, helping people from the business world to unfold and unwrap the stories in their lives. It's very interesting although not very well paid. When this contract runs out, I'll have to search for more work and that's becoming increasingly difficult to find. There's not as much demand for storytellers as there used to be, which is a shame because stories are so, so important.

We struggle with money, in our house. Ronan and Katie are good kids but they always need the latest gear, the latest thing, and we're not all that good at managing money, Annie and I.

So, I hope we'll be chosen for this series. I think we're a good strong family but we could do with a bit of advice about how we could become the perfect family.

Annie Rossi

To be perfectly honest, I'm not sure why I'm writing this. I'm using up precious time when I should be writing another essay. On the form you ask what our hobbies are. I only have one hobby and that's sleeping because the rest of the time I am either packing pork pies, studying, helping with homework, doing the washing or cleaning. I look forward to a time in the future when I have a bit more time for myself and my children. But at the moment I feel as though my life is on hold while I get some qualifications.

   I don't think you can make a perfect family but I'm willing to go along with this because I know that Michael is so enthusiastic about it. It's easy to change a house or a garden but changing a family? I don't think so. Who would be able to tell when that family is perfect? What does 'perfect' mean anyway?

'Mum!' I called at the empty room. 'Why do you have to be really . . . negative?' I felt so irritated with Mum's contribution that I stood up and stamped across the room.

'What's up with you?' Ronan asked as he walked into the room and collapsed onto the sofa. 'Going mad or something?'

'Get up, Ronan!' I shouted. 'I was sitting there.' Ronan moved his feet a few inches out of the way to make a small space for me at the end of the sofa. 'I meant I was *lying* there.'

'Tough! I'm here now,' Ronan replied.

'Get up, Ronan,' I grunted as I tried to push him off the sofa. 'That's my place.'

'No!' Ronan called as he pushed me away.

'Right!' I snapped. I pulled at Ronan's hair to get him off the sofa. I knew it was his Achilles heel.

uch! You animal!' Ronan screeched.

Ronan was just about to thump me when Dad arrived and stood in the kitchen, his arms folded in an angry manner.

'What's going on?' he shouted.

'I was lying on the sofa and Ronan pinched my place,' I said.

'You liar! You've just been attacking me ever since I got in,' Ronan explained. 'Just 'cause you're grumpy about something.'

'No I'm not!'

'Has anyone put the tea on?' Dad boomed. Ronan and I looked at one another. I was tempted to giggle.

'No,' I said, shrugging my shoulders. 'I didn't know what to do.'

'I wrote a note. Look—it's over there on the cooker,' Dad said.

'The cooker?' Ronan laughed. 'I never look at the cooker.'

'Don't be so cheeky, Ronan!' Dad boomed.

'What have you been doing, Katie?' Dad asked.

'I've been reading these,' I confessed.

'What?' Ronan asked.

'The things for the perfect family,' I explained.

'Honestly!' Dad said, bustling around the kitchen, slamming doors and banging down pots and pans. 'I think we can forget all about that,' he snarled. 'If neither of you can be bothered to read a simple note that says, "Take the shepherd's pie out of the freezer and place in the oven at gas mark 6" then I'm sure you won't be able to do as a television producer tells you.'

'Shepherd's pie? Again?' Ronan questioned.

'Don't you dare even *start*, Ronan,' Dad warned, pointing at Ronan with one eye closed.

'Have you had a bad day or something, Dad?' I asked, walking over to the cooker.

'Yes!' he snapped. 'Now get the table ready.'

No please or thank you, no explanation about his bad day. Ronan and I moved quietly around the kitchen, getting things ready. I knew that later, Dad would calm down and apologize and tell us something like he'd received a huge bill this morning and that's what had put him in a bad mood. I also knew that it was best to say nothing about anything. Becoming a perfect family was the last thing on his mind.

The Letter

There was no persuading Dad that evening. There were no apologies or explanations, either. I knew it had something to do with money because when Mum arrived home from work, I heard Dad and her discussing in furious, low voices and then Mum shouted suddenly, 'What do you mean, "I'll need to work overtime"? Why don't *you* get a job in the rotten factory?' Yes, it was definitely to do with money.

That evening I thought about what Isla said about us spending money on the wrong things. In a way she was right—we spent as much on one breakfast at Safeways as we could have done for a fortnight's breakfasts.

I tried not to worry about things like that but sometimes it got me down because we never seem to have enough money for anything and it didn't look as though things would improve for a few years.

It was an automatic thing, putting our application in an envelope and posting it on the way to school. When Dad asked me what I was posting, I said, 'Just a competition from my comic.'

Then I forgot about it. I noticed the days getting a bit longer and I thought about the hedgehogs coming out of hibernation. The weather was sunny and quite warm and that worried me a bit because if the hedgehogs woke up too early they might suffer from severe weather in March. Every morning I escaped to the bottom of the garden to watch for the arrival of a hedgehog.

I did think a little about our *Perfect Families* entry but I wasn't *longing* for a reply or anything. So it was a bit of a surprise when we received a letter on March 7th inviting us for an interview.

I was ecstatic, and Ronan was delighted. After Dad discovered that I'd sent the letter, he was really thrilled, too. He kept saying, 'I've got such a brilliant feeling about this. I'm sure it's the right thing to do.' The thought of the interview seemed to make the house much brighter.

Mum was working back to back shifts in the factory so she didn't hear about it for a few days. When Dad told her, she wasn't pleased. No matter how hard Dad tried to persuade her she was adamant. She wasn't going to the interview.

'What about my work and college? What about school? What about your work? What are you going to do about all this?' Mum demanded to know.

'It'll be *worth* all the disruption,' Dad pleaded. 'I promise you.'

'I'll lose a day's pay, so will you, the kids will miss a day of school . . .' Mum argued. 'You just haven't thought this through, Michael. We can't *manage* without that money!'

Every time Dad raised another reason for going to the interview, Mum said, 'What about . . .' One morning I was so fed up with Mum's 'whatabouts' that I walked to the bottom of the garden, closely followed by Ronan.

'What about . . .' Ronan began and we both laughed. Ronan kicked gravel from the path over the lawn. 'What about what we think?' Ronan complained. 'Nobody seems to be asking us.'

'What's new?' I asked, lifting the twigs at the bottom of each shrub. 'Maybe it's for the best. If Mum doesn't want to do it . . .'

'Yeah, but that's so unfair,' Ronan protested, angrily kicking at the gravel. 'It's three against one—we all want to do it but she doesn't and so she gets her way. That's not fair!'

Back in the kitchen, Dad was almost pleading. 'It's like the lottery—yes, you might waste a pound when you buy a ticket but you have the chance to win millions.'

Mum bustled around the kitchen putting away saucepans and crockery from the day before. 'What are you saying, Mike?' she asked as if she was talking to the shelf.

Dad's hands were frantically pleading as he talked. 'I'm saying, yes, we might lose a day's pay but look at all we might gain . . .'

Still crouching, close to the bottom shelf, Mum turned round abruptly to face Dad. 'What?' she asked. 'What will we gain?'

'Well . . . there's my career, I think it would really help me . . .' Dad began.

'What will I gain?' Mum asked.

'A much better family, I hope,' Dad said, persuasively.

'I doubt it very much,' Mum said, finally. Then she carried on banging about with pots and pans, her mouth set in a determined line. As far as Mum was concerned, nothing more was to be said. They had been like this with one another since they'd had that row about money. Dad told me later that we'd got a massive overdraft, whatever that is.

On the way to school Dad didn't speak much. Not until we met up with Isla. 'Guess what?' Isla trilled.

'What?' I asked flatly, staring straight ahead.

'We're going to be on the telly!' Isla announced.

'What?' Dad asked.

'We're going to be on *Perfect Families*,' Isla said, smiling smugly.

'For definite?' I asked. I tried not to show the envy and disappointment in my face. It was hard because I'm not very good at hiding my feelings.

'Well . . . we've got an interview, next week,' Isla conceded.

Dad looked at me with renewed determination in his eyes. 'That does it,' he said, when we reached the school gate and Isla skipped off.

'What does?' I questioned, quietly.

'We are going to that interview whether your mother likes it or not!' Dad proclaimed.

The Interview

'I must be mad!' Mum said, in an irritated voice. She was examining her reflection in the passenger mirror as we drove to the Summer House Hotel.

'No you're not,' Dad said, soothingly. 'You know this will be good for us.'

'I doubt it . . . but anyway, can we stop for some mints?' Mum asked. 'My mouth's really dry.'

'OK,' Dad agreed.

Mum dashed into the newsagent's. 'How did you persuade her?' Ronan asked, leaning forward. 'The other day she was dead against it.'

'D'you know, Ronan,' Dad said, leaning back and stretching his arm across Mum's seat. 'I presented her with your argument. Three for, one against, isn't fair if she scuppers it all and so on,' Dad explained.

'Brilliant,' I said. Up until that morning we didn't even know if we would be going but Dad had managed to persuade Mum.

'Could only get these soft ones,' Mum said. 'Better than nothing, eh?'

A few minutes later we were there, at the Summer House Hotel. Isla and her parents sat at one end of the foyer. They waved at us politely. There didn't seem to be any other families. 'Aren't you going to speak to Isla?' Mum asked.

'No, it's OK,' I replied. 'I'll see her at school tomorrow.'

Mauritia Venetia, the programme producer, kept us waiting for forty minutes. She walked confidently into the foyer, looking relaxed and glamorous in a tailored grey trouser suit. 'Be with you soon,' she mouthed, dramatically, to Isla's mum and dad.

'Sorry! Good morning, Mr and Mrs Rossi, Katie and Ronan,' she beamed. 'Terribly sorry for the late start. Dreadful, *dreadful* traffic on the M1. What an absolutely awful stretch of motorway. Puts one off commuting altogether.' Then she added quickly, 'How are you all?' But before any of us had a chance to reply she continued, 'So glad you could come today. Right! If you'll follow me . . .'

Mauritia showed us into a small conference room. 'Here we are! Anyone for coffee?' Mauritia asked brightly, promptly pouring a cup for herself. 'Now we'll be in this room for several hours so I want you to really make yourselves at home and . . . just help yourselves to *anything* in here,' Mauritia said.

'Great!' Ronan said, eyeing the baskets of biscuits and chocolates.

'I'm sure you're all dying to know about the series,' she smiled and waited for our response before continuing. Dad nodded vigorously. 'We consider ourselves sort of social designers and decorators. We want to revamp, *redesign* your family in *exactly* the same way we've done with homes and gardens. We want to *mould* you.' Mauritia's hands moved creatively as she spoke. 'We want to shape you into the most *perfect* family unit.'

Mum breathed a deep sigh as if she was already exhausted.

'Great idea, Mauritia,' Dad enthused, his arms moving around like Mauritia's. 'Absolutely love the concept.' Mum glared at Dad as if he was an annoying stranger.

'OK, so . . . we're using research from the Milton Keynes Institute for the Family. The results of this research will form the framework for our series. Right . . . so . . . this is what I want you to do: I want you to discuss how you feel about each of these statements and I will leave the room for a few minutes to give you a chance to talk these things through in private. So . . . I'll leave the door a little ajar, just in case you need me. I'll just be along the corridor with the other family for a few moments . . .' With that, Mauritia tiptoed out of the room as if she had just finished reading a bedtime story.

We all read in total silence.

Making the Perfect Family

- Perfect families are attractive and presentable.

- Perfect families have a good standard of living with at least one parent earning a reasonable wage.

- Perfect families have a good balanced diet with at least one parent being able to cook to a high standard.

- Perfect families live in pleasant surroundings and enjoy their house and garden.

- Perfect families have good links with their extended family and local community.

- Perfect families get on well with one another and enjoy spending time together.

- Perfect families . . . well, what do you think makes a perfect family?

Mum didn't hesitate to express her opinion. 'What a load of rubbish!' she exclaimed, throwing her sheet onto the coffee table. 'I know plenty of families who are positively ugly and they're lovely people and they have perfect lives. I think that's total nonsense!'

'Who do you know who's ugly?' Dad asked, surprised by Mum's reaction.

'Yes, who?' I asked. It was a funny thing for Mum to say.

'Well, you know what I mean. You don't necessarily have to be attractive to be perfect,' Mum said.

'Yes, I suppose you're right but I do think we're imperfect on a few of these things,' Dad said, gesturing towards his sheet.

'Like what?' Mum asked defensively.

'Well, I don't earn a reasonable wage at present and . . .'

'We don't cook very well,' Mum agreed. 'But that doesn't make us *so* imperfect. Plenty of families are like us—living from the freezer to the oven.'

'Talking about food makes me really hungry,' I said. I was a bit bored with everything—it wasn't what I had expected. I stretched out my legs and scratched my head.

'Katie, stop scratching!' Mum said.

'Sorry, Mum,' I said. 'I'm just a bit bored.'

'Me too,' Ronan agreed. 'I thought we'd be playing all sorts of games, like they do on television game shows.'

'Have you got nits *again*?' Mum asked, leaning towards me. 'We've only just finished that blessed treatment.'

'No, I sometimes scratch my head when I'm a bit tired or bored,' I replied.

'Let me have a look,' Mum said. She walked round to my

chair, put her glasses on and pulled my head back. 'Lean back, love.'

I hated it when Mum got into one of these moods and in the Summer House Hotel of all places. 'Leave it, Mum,' I pleaded. 'She could be back any minute.'

'Mum!' Ronan hissed.

'Annie, we're supposed to be discussing this, not looking for little beasties in Katie's hair,' Dad whispered, looking towards the door. 'You're getting a bit obsessed about them.'

'I know but I just want to check Katie's hair. I'm fed up with those blinking nits . . .' Mum argued. 'If they take hold . . .'

'It's those hedgehogs,' Ronan said, leaning back in his chair and swinging round. 'I reckon that's why you get nits so much.'

'They carry fleas, stupid, not head lice!' I snapped. 'Please, Mum, let me sit up.'

'Just one more second,' Mum said, lifting my hair from around my ears.

'Can't I get my hair cut, Mum?' I asked. 'Then I won't get nits so much.'

'No, you can't! I'm not letting you cut your beautiful hair. I always wanted long hair when I was a little girl . . .' Mum replied, wistfully.

'Why can't I grow my hair then?' Ronan asked, dolefully.

'Don't be difficult, Ronan,' Mum said, squeezing Ronan's shoulder as she went past his chair.

'Annie!' Dad snapped.

'What?' Mum shouted back.

'Are we a perfect family or not?' Dad snarled.

There was no chance for any of us to reply because Mauritia bounced back into the room. 'Right everyone. How are you getting on? Could you *become* the perfect family? Let's find out!'

My heart sank. All I could think was, She'll never choose us. She'll *never* choose us!

The Decision

You see, we didn't know what Mauritia was looking for. Was she looking for a family who smiled all the time? Was she looking for a family who were totally miserable? We didn't know. She didn't give anything away when she bounced back into the room. She listened politely and nodded vigorously, especially when Mum voiced her objections. In fact, she was almost agreeing with Mum which made Mum criticize things even more.

I wasn't too worried about Isla's family. Everything was just right in their lives, they were already perfect. In a way I was very envious of Isla because there were never any crises or dramas in her house. Things always ran very smoothly for Isla's family.

In the end, it was a good day out. We had a brilliant lunch—lots of things we don't normally have—and in the afternoon it was much more interesting. We had some puzzles and activities to complete as a family, while two researchers watched how we worked together. Mum relaxed a lot and we were our almost-normal selves. We all thought we'd blown it so we just enjoyed ourselves. On the way home, Mum said that it was the best day she'd had for a while, 'A complete break.'

The next day was March 22nd. It was bitterly cold and freezing rain beat against the windows. It seemed as though the day before hadn't happened, as if it had been blown away by the stormy night. In school, Isla behaved as if she was a film star, surrounded by classmates who wanted to know what it had been like, as though her family were the ones who had been chosen. I talked to Krishna about it but I didn't want to say much to anyone else because I thought we'd blown it.

Then on April 4th, we received a letter from Mauritia. She wanted us on the show! Us? But we had made a mess of the interview. I couldn't understand it. But it was true; printed in black and white, signed by Mauritia. She wanted our family for the series.

Brilliant!

HEARTLANDS TELEVISION
Gable Oak • Nottingham

April 3rd

Dear Mr and Mrs Rossi, Katie and Ronan,

I am truly delighted to inform you that you have been chosen as the family for our series, *So You Want To Be The Perfect Family©*

Congratulations! We would like to start preliminary filming as soon as possible. I know that although you are very keen on the idea of appearing on television for several weeks, you also have some reservations. This is perfectly natural. I would suggest that you discuss these reservations as a family and then let me know, within seven days, if you would like to proceed with this project, before you sign the television contract.

I am looking forward to working with you. I think you truly are an ideal family for *So You Want To Be The Perfect Family©*

Looking forward to hearing from you very soon.

With very best wishes,

Mauritia Venetia

Mauritia Venetia
Series Producer

47

Mauritia said *we* might have reservations. No, *Mum* had reservations. She had reservations enough for all of us. Mauritia said we should *discuss* these reservations. No, we didn't discuss them. Mum shouted them. Every day. For a week.

'Ask yourselves, "why does she want us"?' Mum questioned loudly, as she stomped about the kitchen after coming home from work.

'Well, I think it's because we're an interesting family,' Dad replied, leaning against the door jamb, quite relaxed about everything.

'Well, I don't think it's as simple as that so I'm not doing it,' Mum announced with a stamp of her foot.

'We can't do it without you, Mum,' Ronan protested. He had been lying on the lounge floor, doing his homework, but he wandered into the kitchen when he heard Mum's shouts.

'Well, we can't do it,' Mum said.

I tried to plead with Mum. 'Mum, please think about it.'

'I thought about it before we went for the interview,' Mum said. She was leaning against the sink, looking out of the window with her back to all of us. 'I said I didn't want to go for it. I knew this would happen, that we'd get this far and you would all be disappointed because I didn't want to do it.'

'But you loved the interview,' Dad reminded Mum.

Mum turned around. 'Yes, it was a nice day out, but this is different. This is cameras in our house for weeks and weeks on end and I don't want it.'

'Why not?' I asked, totally fed up with Mum.

'Because I know, I've just got a very strong feeling that it will not be a good thing for us. Don't ask me why, I just know it,' Mum replied.

'How do you know? You're not a fortune teller,' Ronan interrupted, before flouncing out of the room.

'Don't be cheeky, Ronan,' Mum shouted. 'I just don't want our lives splashed all over the television for months on end. Apart from anything else, I've got my A level exams soon,' Mum ranted.

In a way, I'd forgotten about Mum's exams. 'It won't interfere with those, Mum,' I said, trying to reassure her.

'It will and I don't want us on the telly and people seeing how badly I'm doing and . . .'

Dad tried to calm things down. 'Let's leave it,' Dad suggested.

'Yes!' Mum snapped. 'Let's forget all about it.'

'No,' Dad said, calmly. 'Let's leave things for a few days and think about it again.'

'We're running out of time,' I reminded Dad. 'Mauritia said we have to let her know within a week.'

'If they really want us, they'll wait for our decision,' Dad said, knowingly.

And that was that. The excitement of being chosen died down and we all went back to normal for a day or two. I felt very angry and frustrated with Mum, so did Ronan and Dad but we didn't discuss it. Then about three days later Mum came home and announced that she'd changed her mind. Just like that.

We were all amazed. Mum didn't look all that pleased with her decision, more resigned to her fate. This is what had made her change her mind—somehow the boss at her factory had found out about her being chosen for the show. He told Mum that it would mean fantastic free publicity for the pork pie company and so she'd get a huge bonus at the end of the series.

'I don't have much choice,' Mum explained. 'We need this money badly, what with the overdraft and everything.'

'I'll ring Mauritia,' Dad said, relieved.

'I feel like I've sold my soul,' Mum said, with a deep sigh.

'Don't be daft, Mum,' I said, trying to make her feel better. 'It'll be brilliant, you just watch!'

Part Two

Watch The Family

Filming the Family

Dad was absolutely walking on air. He couldn't believe his good fortune. He was going to be on the television. I was quite pleased, too, so was Ronan. Mum retreated into her studying and the pork pie factory. They suddenly thought that she was the best thing since instant pastry and we were getting lots of complimentary pork pies for tea.

Dad rang Mauritia with our decision.

HEARTLANDS TELEVISION
Gable Oak • Nottingham

April 14th

Dear Michael, Annie, Ronan, and Katie,
  So pleased that you have decided to take part in the series. Our researchers will be visiting your house and local community within the next few days to gather some more background material. Then we'll be ready to start. Try not to worry about preparing anything for the filming. We want things to be as natural and ordinary as possible.
  Here's to a *brilliant* series,

Mauritia

So, we were going to be on the telly. Mauritia asked each one of us to keep a detailed written diary to be used as a follow-up to the series. (Mauritia said that our diaries might be published as a sort of Christmas tie-in.) I asked Mum and Dad and Ronan if I could use their diaries to help tell my story of how we became really, really famous.

Mum was a bit reluctant. She didn't write much during the first few weeks because she was seriously revising for her exams. Dad and Ronan have written loads.

This is what Ronan thought of the first week of filming:

Ronan's Diary

Monday April 30th

This is the day they start making us into the perfect family. This is wicked cool, this book that Mauritia's given me for keeping my diary. It's got all facts and figures about running. I could sit and read it all day. Mum's going to be followed by the cameras today. Hope she doesn't keep going on about how much revision she's got to do for her exams and all that sort of stuff.

Tuesday May 1st

Dad had the cameras today. Bet that was exciting. Not! Storytelling, supermarket, swimming, fetching Katie from school. Hope people don't fall off their settees in a coma watching that. We're in the local paper—now we're celebrities. I've cut it out. All the kids at school keep asking me about it and stuff. Think it's going to be wicked. I'm gonna be famous.

Wednesday May 2nd
Now it's my turn with the cameras today. Washed my hair, spent ages in the bathroom— they're not allowed in there. Wish I didn't have that spot on my forehead—it's about to explode.

   Terry, the cameraman who was with me for a day, filmed me in English. Miss Marinski dressed up like a film star and she was acting all hard like she was the toughest teacher in the universe.

   Running club at dinner time. Majorly embarrassing—Terry wanted to follow me into changing rooms so he could film me with my mates getting changed. 'No way!' I said. He stayed outside. Watched me doing cross country which I didn't mind cause I'm so fantastic at it. After that he let me have a go with the camera.

Thursday

Katie's turn to be followed today. Bet she'll bore Terry to bits talking about hedgehogs and hoglets.

After school, we all had to travel to the studio in Nottingham in a seriously posh car, to say what we hoped to get from this series. Dad said, I believe in this family. I know we can be a perfect family because we've got everything going for us—we just need a little advice and support like all families. Like . . . what?

So . . . why do I want it? Simple. I want everyone to know what a brilliant runner I am. And I just like the idea of being on telly and everybody noticing me and saying what a cool guy I am. Shame about the spot, wish it would go. Couldn't say all that, Mauritia wouldn't let me—especially the bit about the spot.

Monday nights were *Perfect Family* nights on the television. I've kept the television section for that day. This is how it looked in the paper.

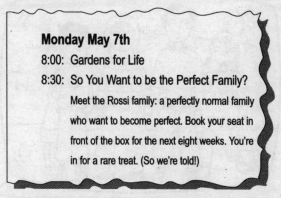

Monday May 7th
8:00: Gardens for Life
8:30: So You Want to be the Perfect Family?
Meet the Rossi family: a perfectly normal family
who want to become perfect. Book your seat in
front of the box for the next eight weeks. You're
in for a rare treat. (So we're told!)

So, we switched on to watch ourselves. I had a really weird feeling inside. There were the opening credits and then, it was us. Marianna Clancy, the bubbly presenter, spoke first: 'Good Evening! Welcome to an Exciting New Series, *So You Want To Be The Perfect Family*. This is the ultimate in make-over programmes. In the next few weeks we are going to meet a very special family who will be transformed into the Perfect Family.' The presenter then hesitated for a meaningful moment. 'So tonight I'd like to give a very warm welcome to the Rossi family from the Midlands!'

'She looks a lot better on the telly,' Ronan said.

'And she's not so grumpy,' Mum said. 'Oh—I can't believe it! Don't we look different on the telly?' Mum had been a bit more positive about everything since we'd been to the studio.

'Yes!' I agreed. It was extremely cringe-worthy. 'It's so embarrassing.'

'Shush!' Ronan snapped.

'Welcome, Michael, Annie, Ronan, and Katie, the Rossi family! Now there are a lot of people out there who are probably thinking, you must be mad putting yourselves through this. So, tell me, Michael: why are you trying to be the perfect family?'

'Well, Marianna, we're a good family but we want to be better. It's as simple as that,' Dad responded.

'Annie—the mum of this lovely family—a little bird has told me that at first you were a little reluctant about this whole project. How are you feeling about it now?'

'I'm really pleased we're doing it, Marianna. I think most mothers would be worried about anything which exposes their family life but we've talked about it and we're a strong family so I think we'll be really good for this.'

'Do you think you'll survive?' Marianna asked impishly.

'I'm sure we will,' Mum replied confidently.

'This is Ronan, he's thirteen and you're really looking forward to all this, aren't you Ronan?'

'Yes, I think this will be brilliant,' Ronan said in words prepared over hours and hours.

'What about you, Katie, how do you feel about everything?' Marianna asked.

'Well . . . I'm the youngest in our family and I'm really glad that we're doing this,' I said. I had been told what to say.

'Katie, is it hard being the littlest?' Marianna asked, with a sweet smile, as if I was only two years old.

'Mmm . . . sometimes,' I replied. 'But they say the best things come in small packages.' I felt so embarrassed. It didn't even sound like me. It wasn't one of my sayings. 'Switch it off! Switch it off!' I called.

'What's the best thing about your family, Katie?' Marianna Clancy asked looking sweetly into my face.

'The best thing is Mum and Dad cos they look after us so well . . .' I said. I had actually been *told* to say that mainly because I didn't understand the question and I hadn't a clue what to say.

'Michael, you sound almost like the perfect family already! How do you think you can improve?'

'No family's perfect, Marianna, as you well know yourself,' Dad replied.

'Tell me about it,' Marianna said, smiling even more broadly. 'It's so very hard being a parent these days. Annie, do you think there's *any* room for improvement?'

'Lots and lots, Marianna. That's exactly why we volunteered for this!'

'So—that's the Rossi family from the Midlands. Over the next few weeks we'll be showing them how their family life can become perfect. But first, let's have a little look at the Rossi family at home and at work.'

'Oh no,' Ronan groaned. 'This is the worst bit, they'll see my spot.'

'We'll see what we looked like when the cameras followed us all around for the week,' Dad said.

'Yes, prepare to be embarrassed,' Mum replied, lifting herself off the saggy sofa. 'Whilst the adverts are on, I'll make us a cuppa.'

'Put a little something in mine, will you? I think I'm going to need it!' Dad said. The cameras watched as we all went about our *normal* business. It was really, really strange, watching ourselves trying to be normal. It seemed as though nothing was really normal any more.

Normal became a thing of the past. When you read my diary and see what happened to Dad the next day, you'll see why.

Changing the Family

HEARTLANDS TELEVISION
Gable Oak • Nottingham

May 7th

Dear Michael, Annie, Ronan, and Katie,
Superb start to the series. Enclosed are all the
press cuttings. Read and . . . enjoy. They love
you. So . . . are we ready for the next stage,
'Happy Families are Attractive and Presentable'?
I know that this will be absolutely *brilliant*.
You are *so* right for this series.
   Pascal will be with you on Tuesday morning,
first thing. He is an absolute darling and an
expert on personal make-overs. He'll make you
look totally wonderful. I won't recognize you
when I see you!
   Have an excellent week,

Mauritia

Pascal did arrive on Tuesday. He wasn't an absolute
darling, whatever that means. I know that Ronan hates my
sayings but as far as Pascal was concerned, 'All that glitters
isn't gold'.

My Diary by Katie

Tuesday May 8th

First thing—I put milk out for the hedgehog. Sometimes wonder why I'm doing it. The garden is a hedgehog-free zone and I can't believe that after all this time none have appeared. Still, had a brill day at school. Everyone was asking about the programme. They all like it.

Back home, Dad was sitting at the table with his head in his hands, looking really fed up. He said that Pascal, the man who came to make us look better, has really upset him. I tried to tell him that it doesn't matter what you look like, it's what's inside that matters but he just groaned.

Later on I heard him telling Mum about Pascal. Pascal told Dad that he has to go into a clinic to have a hair transplant. (It's like a heart transplant or a kidney transplant only with hair.) Pascal says that no one should be bald in this day and age. At first Mum was really laughing about it but then she calmed down and said, 'That's ridiculous! It's really trendy to be bald.' And Dad said, 'But I'm not BALD!' Then Mum said, 'I never said you were. I meant ...' And Dad said, 'It's too late, the damage is done now!'

Wednesday
At the bottom of our garden there are a million slugs and if we had a hedgehog she would be so happy because there's so much food but no hedgehogs have appeared. I just don't know why. Isla was really horrible to me at morning play because she said I was getting too big-headed about being on the telly. But I'm not. Krishna says that Isla's jealous because her family wanted to be on it but they didn't pass the interview. On the way home Isla apologized, (which is a rare thing) and she said, 'Can I come to your house one day when the cameras are there?' I knew she was only saying that because she wanted to be on the telly but in a way I didn't care.

Mum was in a funny sort of mood this evening. She told us about her meeting with Pascal. He said she was two stone overweight and he said she had to go to a gym and a slimming club. She said, 'When am I going to get time to go to a gym?' He said, 'You'll have to make time. Some people go at six o'clock in the morning.' She said, 'Some people have to work in pork pie factories at six o'clock in the morning.'

Then Pascal said that she had to cut her beautiful long hair. Mum's not bothered about that which I think is really strange. She said she wants a trendy new style. I can't believe Mum's changed her mind so quickly. She always wanted lovely long hair. I'm really surprised at the way Mum's taken to this, in fact it feels a bit strange. She's changed her mind so suddenly. It makes me wonder if she's all right.

Thursday
Dad and Pascal met me at the gate after school and on the way home the cameras filmed me and

Pascal walking along and chatting. Pascal walks like his feet are landing on cushions and he talks to me as if he's one of my mates and makes daft jokes. Then he said to me, 'What d'you think of the way you look, Katie?' And I said, 'It's not how you look, it's what's inside that matters.' Pascal thought that was funny and he said, 'You don't really mean that, do you, Katie?' so I said, 'Yes. You shouldn't judge a book by its cover.' He asked me about five times. Then he was all quiet for a few minutes and they stopped filming and Pascal went away with his head in his hands.

We went to a really trendy hairdresser's in town and Pascal sat me in the consultation area and said, 'Katie- you're almost twelve years old and you look about eight. How would you like to look cool and trendy like other children of your age?' Dad was sitting next to Pascal and he said, 'I think that's a bit unfair.' Then Dad and Pascal had this quiet argument and Pascal started getting cross.

Pascal came back and they

started filming. He stood in front of me and said, firmly, 'Katie, this hair will have to go and I'm going to see if you can visit an orthodontist to have your teeth straightened. Then what do you say we have a look at the smart shops and buy some cool clothes for you?'

I actually wanted my hair cut the other week when Mum thought I had nits again but I didn't like Pascal telling me it had to be done so I said, 'I don't want my hair cut and I like my teeth the way they are.' Dad said, 'Katie' like he was pleading and Pascal said, 'I'll do a wonderful haircut for you, Katie.' But I still said, 'No thanks.' (It was partly because I thought he might find nits in my hair) Pascal started to growl like a dog that's been kept inside for too long. 'Fine, fine, I surrender,' Pascal said.

Me and Dad walked home without talking which is unusual and it made me feel very sad.

Friday
Mum got up early and was eating

chocolate for breakfast. She said, 'I'm starting my diet today so I want to make sure I have lots of energy for college.' Mum went to the hairdresser's with Pascal and she had her hair cut. She is really pleased with it and she kept swinging her hair from side to side to show us how it looked. She's going to the gym, too. Pascal was much happier. He thinks that when we're more attractive, we'll be almost perfect. I'm not sure about that.

Tuesday May 15th
Last night on *Perfect Families*, they showed us with Pascal, being made more attractive. It made me cringe, really cringe.

At school someone left a note on my desk:

> Your dad's bald,
> Your mum's fat,
> Ronan's bad and
> You're SAD.
> Signed, everyone.

My stomach dropped and my head hurt. Is this what it's like to be famous?

Working the Family

Dad's Diary

Tuesday May 15th

On Tuesday evening, Justin popped in to see us. Who's Justin? Justin is a Celebrity Employment Adviser and he had been commissioned by Heartlands Television to make us into a Perfect <u>Working</u> Family. 'I'm just reading from the programme notes here,' he said . . . 'Perfect Families have a good standard of living with at least one parent earning a reasonable wage.'

Justin was due to arrive at ten o'clock on Tuesday morning. At midday he rang to say he was dealing with an emergency. An emergency? What <u>emergencies</u> do Celebrity Employment Advisers have to deal with. No champagne in the workers' fridge? Burst pipes in the golf club? Shortage of caviar for the butties?

So, I was not best pleased when Justin arrived, just as I was grilling sausages and bacon for dinner. Justin <u>looked</u> like a celebrity. He was dressed in an expensive continental suit, shirt, and tie. When he sat down in the kitchen he glared at the grill as if it was offending him.

'Could we sit in another room?' he asked. 'It's just that . . .' and then he started to smell his jacket as if it had gone off.

'No, Justin, my kids need to eat and I've got to cook the tea,' I quickly replied. But I wasn't concentrating on anything properly. I wanted to do this interview, I wanted to go along with the spirit of the thing but I was cross at being kept waiting for so long. For much of the interview Justin was talking to my back and the cameras rolled, all the time.

'Let me get this straight,' Justin began, reading from his notes. 'Mum's at college, doing A levels as well as working part-time; Michael, you have a job as a storyteller. So how do you manage . . . financially?'

'With difficulty, but we manage. My wage isn't too bad,' I said.

'You earn a wage?' Justin asked, incredulously.

'Yes,' I said, nodding. The cheeky pup! Who did he think he was?

'Telling stories?' Justin asked. 'What, exactly is a storyteller? What does a storyteller do?'

I explained to Justin all about storytelling but I could tell by the way his eyes glazed over and the way he tapped his pen on the table that he wasn't impressed. He said as much. 'It isn't a proper job.' That got me. I turned off the grill and sat at the table next to Ronan, who was more than a little impressed with Justin.

'A storyteller tells stories and, yes, I earn money,

real money as a storyteller,' I replied, a little impatiently.

'But that's not a proper job,' Justin sneered.

'What is a proper job, Justin?' I asked him. 'Is yours a proper job? I mean, what do you really do?' I knew I was being a bit aggressive but he deserved it.

Justin shuffled uncomfortably in his chair. 'I'm a Celebrity Employment Adviser.'

'And what, exactly, is a Celebrity Employment Adviser?' I questioned.

'A Celebrity Employment Adviser advises celebrities about work,' Justin said, then he shuffled his papers into a neat pile. Justin seemed to be very aware of the cameras rolling and although he was finding me a difficult customer, (probably because I wasn't a celebrity) he was trying hard not to overreact. Justin cleared his throat. 'Mr Rossi, I have advised former popstars and footballers about their future employment. I have worked alongside royalty and travelled abroad extensively . . .'

Then Ronan became a bit more interested. 'Have you? Where have you been?'

'That's not the point,' Justin snapped, focusing on his papers. Ronan looked really hurt at Justin's sharpness. 'The point is this—Heartlands Television have commissioned me to talk to you about your future employment contracts and . . . can we switch the cameras off for a minute?' he yelled. He was really feeling the strain. He loosened his tie and wiped the nervous beads of sweat from his forehead.

'Look, Mr Rossi,' he began again. I told him to call me Michael or even Mike. 'Look, Mike, we have to find you something that earns a proper wage. A proper job.'

Katie wandered into the kitchen and asked when dinner would be ready so I stood up and switched the grill back on. 'That's fine,' I said. 'But I'd like you to know that storytelling is a proper job.'

'Well, we'll have to agree to differ on that,' Justin said. 'Let's get you sorted.' I wasn't happy at Justin's tone of voice or his approach. He looked about eighteen and he was telling me that my storytelling wasn't a proper job. 'I'd just like to remind you that you have signed a legal contract with Heartlands Television to . . .'

In a way, he was threatening me, I knew it. I had too much on my mind and sausages and bacon on the grill. So I gave in.

'Any ideas in mind?' I sighed, resigned to my fate.

Of course, he had loads of ideas. 'Well, I called into a few employment agencies and I think I have just the job for you,' Justin said, gaining confidence with every word.

'So,' I said with a heavy heart. 'When do I start?'

Wednesday May 16th

Yesterday. It was only yesterday that we were sitting at the table at teatime listening to Justin. Dad wasn't listening properly and he wasn't cooking the tea properly which is probably why I was spewing up in the night.

This morning I felt so rough that I didn't even go down to look for the hedgehogs. I just put my head on the table and stared at Ronan eating his big plate of cereal. Mum was anxious about me being poorly. 'You'll just have to cancel your appointment with Justin,' she said to Dad.

'OK,' Dad said. 'It can wait if Katie's ill.' He wasn't bothered about the meeting because Justin wasn't very kind to him about his job.

Mum was worried about missing any time from college and she kept saying, 'This is a critical time for me.'

I crawled on to the settee and sipped at my lemonade which is all we're allowed when we're sick. I looked at the circles on the ceiling while Dad rang Justin. Then I counted all the spiders' webs hanging down and floating in the air like grey decorations. There were loads. I only notice things like that when I'm sick and too tired to read so I just look up at the ceiling or study the pattern on the wallpaper. But the patterns are sort of fading.

Then Dad came into the room with a really long face. He said that Justin said he couldn't cancel the appointment because of the filming timetable so . . . 'What am I going to do with you?' Dad didn't say it like I was a nuisance or anything but like it was a real . . . dilemma. 'I'll come with you, Dad,' I said. 'I am feeling a bit better.'

So I brought the bright turquoise sick bucket from the bathroom to Dad's interview and then to where he was going to work. They showed Dad into this massive room and introduced him to his boss and she said, 'Oh, we can't have children in here,' but she didn't say it when the cameras were switched on. And she said it like people say, 'No smoking in here'.

As if I was a health hazard or something. Charming!

Dad said, 'She's not like a puppy, you know. She knows how to behave herself and if she feels sick she'll vomit into her own bucket and you won't have to clear anything up!'

That made me feel a bit better but the cameraman said I had to stay out of shot while Dad did his trial at the job and that made me feel sort of yucky again.

If he actually gets it, I don't think Dad will last very long at this job. It's just ringing people up and talking all the time.

That's not really a job.

Friday May 18th

In a way it's quite interesting . . . . and exciting, this whole telly thing. I love watching the director and then seeing the way the camera crew get themselves set up. And the fact that everything behind the camera is so untidy, well, compared with what you actually see. It's almost a form of conjuring.

I can tell Katie and Ronan are fascinated by it. Katie had a bit of a bonus this week, in a strange sort of way. She couldn't go to school as she was sick and so she had to come with me to my new job. I wasn't looking forward to it.

The new job is as a telesalesperson for a major kitchen fitting company. I have to persuade innocent people that they desperately need the latest innovations in kitchen design. I've been working there three days now and I have to admit that I really like it. This is how it works. The computer dials several numbers and I speak to the first person who answers and the very first person who answered was . . . . Mrs McPherson of Leeds.

'Good morning, Mrs McPherson,' I said, brightly. 'And how are you on this lovely morning?'

''Tain't lovely here. It's raining,' she replied, gloomily. Then, before I could get a word in she continued, 'And I'm having terrible trouble with my teeth. They've been that bad I feel like suing my dentist. Suing him. He's flaming good for nothing. They don't fit properly, they make me mouth all sore, and they look blooming awful. I feel like ringing the police about him he's put me through that much agony . . .'

She paused for breath. 'Maybe a new kitchen would cheer you up?' I interrupted.

'A new kitchen? How could that make my teeth feel better?' As she spoke I could hear the teeth slipping about in her mouth.

'We have some lovely new kitchens on offer this month and we're actually working in your area at the moment so we'd like to give you the opportunity to meet one of our representatives who can give you a computer generated picture of your new kitchen and a quote. What do you think, Mrs McPherson?' Silence. 'Mrs McPherson?' She just listened as I continued. 'All you have to say is yes or no. When would it be convenient for our kitchen representative to visit your house?' I asked, excitedly, aware that if I arranged a visit I would be paid a bonus.

'This ain't my house,' Mrs McPherson said.

'Oh,' I sighed.

'I'm looking after it for our Maureen, my daughter-in-law. I have to feed her cats every morning. It's a right carry on . . .'

Suddenly the supervisor was standing next to me. 'Cut,' she said. She drew her finger across her throat several times like a manic film director.

'Mrs McPherson,' I said, 'I'll have to go. My supervisor wants a word with me.'

'I thought you said you were a kitchen fitter!' she pleaded.

'Gotta go, bye!'

'Do you know any good dentists?' she cried.

'Mr Rossi,' the supervisor said, with a deep sigh. 'I think you'll need some training. We're not the social services, you know.' She started to walk away and then turned back. 'And you're not a dentist's receptionist!'

Maybe I do need some training but I like this job. I'm getting some great stories! The only trouble is, I'm not getting all that much done in the house because of the strange hours I have to work and I'm not seeing much of Ronan and Katie. I can't see how working in this job makes us into a perfect family.

We shall see.

Family Cooking

On Saturday morning, Orlandia arrived. She was the specialist chef and nutritionist who was going to change our cooking and eating habits, so Mauritia said. Orlandia floated into the house just after breakfast when the kitchen was at its worst. We introduced ourselves and then she started talking to the camera crew. 'She's very, very thin,' Mum whispered. 'Not exactly a brilliant advert for a nutritionist.'

Then the cameras started rolling and Orlandia turned towards us with a strange expression on her face. 'I need to look into your eyes,' she announced.

'What?' Mum asked. It was early days but I could already tell that she wasn't impressed with Orlandia. Then Mum sort of slipped out of the kitchen, she was very busy with her revision.

'The eyes are the windows of the soul,' I said, even though I didn't really know what it meant. I'd seen it on a calendar in Krishna's house.

'Katie!' Ronan sighed.

'And the stomach, funnily enough,' Orlandia agreed. 'The whites of your eyes tell me a great deal about your diet. So . . . I'm going to check each one of you in turn.'

After she'd looked into our eyes, Orlandia announced, 'As I suspected. Your diets are very poor. Not malnourished or anything but they could be a lot better.' We all just stood there and nodded. 'So . . . let's have a look at your food cupboard and fridge freezer. And we'll talk about cooking. Remember—Perfect Families have a good balanced diet with at least one member being able to cook to a high standard.'

Orlandia emptied out the contents of most of the cupboards and then announced, 'OK, I'm going to suggest which items can stay and which can be thrown out.' Dad stared in amazement as Orlandia began to throw food into a black bin bag.

Mum heard the noise and charged back into the kitchen. 'Hang on, hang on!' she shouted. 'What d'you think you're doing?'

'What are you doing? Why are you throwing out so much stuff?' Ronan echoed.

'I could give some of it to my hedgehogs,' I suggested. I didn't like to see all that food going to waste. 'Waste not, want not.'

'It would poison your hedgehogs,' Orlandia asserted. 'And most of it is slowly poisoning you!'

'What, even tomato ketchup?' Ronan asked.

'Yes—even tomato ketchup,' Orlandia replied.

'But I love ketchup,' Ronan protested. 'And burgers, and you can't throw away those mini pizzas and my favourite blue ice-lollies!'

'Oh my goodness,' Orlandia sighed. 'I fear we have a great deal of re-education to do here.'

'What do you mean?' Mum asked, angrily. She had her hands on her hips which, I knew, meant trouble.

'I mean,' Orlandia emphasized, 'that you are clearly

eating a lot of rubbish at present. For example, why are there so many pork pies in your fridge?'

'Because I work in a pork pie factory,' Mum replied, sharply.

'And if you worked in a pet food factory, would you bring samples home for your family to eat?' Orlandia questioned. She stood with her hands outstretched like an irate teacher.

'How dare you!' Mum growled. 'Pork pies are very nutritious.'

'They are not!' Orlandia snapped. 'They are dangerously full of cholesterol.'

Mum was very close to exploding. 'What?' she shouted.

'Annie, remember the cameras,' Dad advised, quietly.

'Can't you switch them off?' Mum snapped.

The cameraman shook his head. I could tell that he was really enjoying this row.

'How dare you come into my house and tell me that there's a load of rubbish in our food cupboards?' Mum shouted, pacing about the kitchen like a lioness guarding her territory.

'I know it hurts, Annie, but we're trying to improve your diet and the general standard of cuisine in this household . . .' Orlandia said, more soothingly. Mum stared angrily at Orlandia. 'And, Mrs Rossi, you did actually volunteer for the series, remember?'

'We didn't volunteer to be insulted!' Mum snapped again.

'I'm not insulting you, Annie, honestly I'm not but you must admit—what you have in your store cupboards and freezer leaves a lot to be desired, doesn't it?'

'But if we like it, that's all that matters,' I suggested. 'There's no accounting for taste.' I couldn't see what Orlandia was getting at.

'Not if it's *so* unhealthy,' Orlandia said in a patronizing manner.

'That's it! I've had enough of this,' Mum fumed. 'I'm going back to my revision.' She stormed out of the kitchen and banged the door loudly behind her.

'I'd better see if she's all right,' Dad fussed, following her quietly out of the kitchen.

'So—Katie and Ronan, that leaves you two in charge of the cooking. Who wants to be the one?' Orlandia asked.

'Boys don't do cooking,' Ronan said.

'Neither do girls, Ronan,' I said. He was only saying that because cooking is too much like hard work.

'Some of the best cooks in the land are boys, Ronan. It's really, really cool to be good at cooking, honestly,' Orlandia enthused.

'Is it?' Ronan asked, hesitantly.

'Yes. It's so, so cool to be good in the kitchen,' Orlandia repeated. 'Did you know that since the Manchester United footballers have been having cooking lessons in the afternoons, they're selling red aprons in sport shops. It has really helped the team on the football field. *Cooking* is the *new* football!'

I could see Ronan's mind working. It was very easy to persuade him and Orlandia had said just the right thing. 'OK then. Where do you want me to start?' Ronan volunteered.

Orlandia was delighted with her conversion. 'Let's get the cupboards sorted out first, kids, and then we'll get down to some seriously cool cooking!'

Ronan's Diary

Saturday May 19th

It's cool to cook. It's cool to cook. It's cooool to cook, man!

Somebody's got to do it. Somebody has to learn. Mum went upstairs in a major huff because Orlandia says we eat rubbish. Dad went after Mum. She's started storming out of the room and the more she does it the more Mauritia rubs her hands together in glee. Because it's good television.

Anyway, I am learning cooking. Orlandia brought this wicked outfit like one of those celebrity chefs on the telly. (And all the Man Utd players.) Katie's got one too.

Me and Orlandia emptied the freezer of all the burgers and sausages and fish fingers. Katie tut-tutted like an old woman. Wanted to give the burgers to her hedgehogs (that don't exist). If I put these burgers at the end of the garden, I'll definitely get hedgehogs, she whinged but Orlandia thinks she'll only get rats because only rats eat such rubbish.

Orlandia said we had to try and cheer up Mum and Dad with some wicked cooking but first we had to go shopping. Orlandia had to

check if it was OK to take us to the
supermarket. Mum wanted to know who was
paying. Anyway, at the supermarket, Orlandia
took ages. She squeezed nearly every
vegetable. She bought stuff I'd never even
heard of. She's got a well cool car, Orlandia.
With a convertible roof. It will look well cool on
the telly when my mates see me and Katie in it.

Back home. Get your sleeves rolled up, we're
going to start cooking, she says. So I put on my
cool new cooking gear with black and white
trousers and white top. Then we start cooking.
Let's start off, Orlandia says with . . . boiling
an egg. Boiling an egg? I say. That's not
cooking, that's just putting an egg in water and
switching on the stove.

That's cooking, she says, smiling like I'm
daft. We're going to make a wonderful salad.
Katie says, salad's not cooking, it's definitely
not cooking. Salad's what you have in the
summer when you don't want to cook. Then
Orlandia smiled at Katie and ruffled her hair
like she was daft, too. What's cooking?
Orlandia asked. It's pies and potatoes and
gravy, I said and Katie says it's putting stuff

in the oven. And what do you do with it before
you put it in the oven? Orlandia asks again.
Take it out of the packet, Katie says. Orlandia
says if you're really cooking, you can't just take
things out of a packet and stuff them in the
oven.

We made some bread to go with the salad.
It's well cool making bread. Well cool! Me and
Katie thumped it and folded it over and
shouted names at it as we made it smaller.
It's wicked, making bread, absolutely wicked!

Called Mum and Dad for lunch. Come and
get it! I shouted. It took them ages and ages
to get to the table. It's ready, I shouted
again and I thought, ungrateful brats. Had to
shout at them a third time. What took you so
long? I shouted. We've been waiting ages! Now
you know how I feel when I've cooked dinner
and you don't come at once, Mum said.
Miserable or what? But . . . . after a few
mouthfuls she was seriously smiling. This is lovely,
Ronan. Then she stood up and kissed me. I did
it, too, Katie protested.

It's well cool, cooking. I wouldn't mind doing
it every day, if they let me.

Friday May 25th

I'm learning to cook. So is Ronan but he's only doing it because he likes the outfit Orlandia bought for him. Mine is too big. I have to roll up the legs and turn over the sleeves. The first thing we did with Orlandia was make a salad with boiled eggs and funny oily fishes. I think they're called anchorveys. They're good for your brain and they help you to live longer. I wonder if hedgehogs would like them?

Ronan is getting big headed. He thinks because he can make bread he can do anything. The next thing we did with Orlandia was to make a special Sunday dinner. Orlandia said Mum and Dad could go out while we cooked. Sunday dinner is so hard to cook. That's why we never have it. Ronan made notes so he could do dinner next week all by himself. Orlandia came in all week, after we'd got home from school, to show me and Ronan how to do the cooking. I didn't mind. Well, not much. It should be Mum and Dad who are doing the cooking but Dad is too busy selling kitchens and Mum is trying so hard for her exams as well as working in the factory.

But other mums and dad's do the cooking. Why can't mine do it?

When the cooking bit was on the telly, Mum just looked angry all the time. Isla said my mum and dad are lazy for not doing the cooking. Krishna said her mum said that my mum should do all the cooking and work in the house. She says, 'A woman's place is in the home.' I'm fed up arguing with them about it. It's been a really hard week at school.

Thing is, I agree with Isla and Krishna. Mum and Dad should be doing the cooking, not me and Ronan, but I won't say that any more.

Mauritia keeps saying, 'We're nearly halfway there—Ronan and Katie, you're stars. People love to see children getting involved in the kitchen.'

That made me feel a bit better. A bit.

There was another note on my table. It said:

> There's nits in your hair,
> fleas in your chair,
> poison in your pantry.
> No wonder you're ugly!

I wonder who wrote it?

HEARTLANDS TELEVISION
Gable Oak • Nottingham

26th May

Dear Michael, Annie, Ronan, and Katie,
  Congratulations, once again! Absolutely wonderful programme on cooking. Isn't Orlandia fantastic?
  You are such wonderful people for this programme. Just a v. quick note to let you know that we have managed to secure the services of . . . McCartney Stephens for the next stage, 'Perfect Families Live in Pleasant Surroundings and Enjoy their House and Garden'. He is the absolute Michelangelo of interior design and I know he will be tremendous for your home and for the programme. McCartney would like a short statement from all of you about your home. He has watched the programmes, he thinks you're tremendous characters and he is so excited about working with you.
  Enjoy the transformation of your home,
  Best . . .

Mauritia

These are the statements we wrote for McCartney Stephens. (What a name!) At the time, Mum was just about to start her A level exams and Dad was . . . too busy.

Katie

This is what I like about my home—the garden, because at the bottom of the garden there are no houses or roads but just a brook and I know that we get lots of wildlife in our garden because of this. It sometimes gets a bit untidy in the house and this makes me cross if one of my friends comes to visit, especially if it's Isla. Dad keeps piles and piles of newspapers for weeks just in case there's a good story in them and Mum leaves her books all over the house. And nobody ever seems to put the clean washing away.

I like the lounge where Mum says we all collapse into a heap but the sofa is very saggy and uncomfortable. I like my room but I would like some new wallpaper because I feel that I have grown out of the Peter Rabbit wallpaper and quilt cover, even though it has almost faded off the material. (That shows how old it is.) Mum says that she's kept the Peter Rabbit wallpaper because she

---

knows how much I like wildlife. But Peter Rabbit isn't really wildlife, is he? (And I am almost twelve years old)

There are lots of things I would like to change about our house but Mum and Dad say that we don't ever have enough money to start so we might as well leave it. But now that Dad has got a proper job, (even though he doesn't think it's a proper job) we might have more money. Mum doesn't want anything doing because it will disturb her whilst she's studying.

Sometimes when I go to Isla's house I feel a bit jealous because she has lovely comfy sofas and bright wallpaper and it's always tidy. Isla's mum is always tidying up the house — it's like a hobby for her. I sometimes wish my mum, or even Dad, had a hobby like this. I would like someone who can tidy up after us. But Mum says we should tidy up after ourselves.

Our House by Ronan

Dear McCartney,

Just a few things about our house. Now that I'm becoming an expert at cooking I think we should have a new kitchen. It's all right if you're just taking things out of the freezer all the time but if you are cooking proper meals you need to have a fully equipped kitchen. I tried to talk to my parents about this but they won't listen. Mum says, I can't believe that you're saying this Ronan, because I've had to put up with that blessed place for so many years and now, because you can boil an egg you think we should have a new kitchen!

So it doesn't look like we'll get a new kitchen. The second thing we need is a room we could convert into a home gym and next to that a sauna for sports injuries. But I might as well think of flying to Jupiter. Dad says that no matter what you've got you're never satisfied with your own home, which might be right. I am not satisfied with our house at all. It is a dump. There's lots of things need doing to put it right but we haven't got enough money and nobody in this house has any time to put it right. Things are always breaking as well, just when you need them. Like the microwave. It has been broken for about two years and nobody has bothered to fix it. Now Mum just uses the microwave door as a mirror!

Maybe we should just move house. Can we?

The house was upside down when McCartney Stephens arrived—early. In fact, no one was out of bed. Mum, in her dressing gown, started to run around and panic but Dad was quite cool and calm. He didn't seem to notice that the sofa was covered in clean washing that had needed sorting for about three days.

Dad answered the door in his blue and yellow pyjamas. 'You're very welcome,' he said, holding out his hand for McCartney to shake.

'Thank you,' McCartney said, looking at Dad as if he had two heads. Then he looked into the hall and cried, 'Oh, wow! What a house!' He sort of pirouetted into the hall as if taking everything in.

'What?' Ronan exclaimed.

'What a house,' McCartney Stephens repeated, with his arms outstretched. 'I simply love this house already . . . It is *so* last century.'

'What?' Mum and Dad asked, rooted to the spot with amazement.

'It is so, *so* last century. I love it when I get to work on a house like this. I treat it as my blank canvas where I can start from scratch. Go back to basics and refurbish, reshape every room into a living reality for . . .' McCartney's arms waved about in the air, as though he was already painting his canvas.

'What do you mean, it's so last century?' Mum questioned, the smile vanishing from her face. Her arms were folded in a determined manner.

'Well, it just is, dear,' McCartney said, placing his hands on Mum's shoulders.

Mum shrugged McCartney's arms away and walked

down the hall towards the kitchen. 'You make us sound like the Victorians or something,' she said.

'That was the century before, dear,' McCartney said, with a sigh, following Mum. 'Your house is very mid to late twentieth century.'

'What do you mean by that?' Ronan asked, when we were all in the lounge waiting for McCartney to continue.

'Well . . . put simply, it's *very* dated but . . . for all that, it's very twee. I mean, you don't see many, if any, sofas like that any more,' McCartney said. He didn't seem to see the pile of last century clothes all over it. Mum cleared them quickly and put them on a chair in the kitchen. Half the pile fell on to the floor.

'So what are you saying, McCartney?' Mum asked as she flopped into the saggiest bit of the sofa. 'Is it valuable?'

'Hardly,' McCartney said, sniffing. 'By the way, please call me Mac.' He sat gingerly at one end of the sofa.

'Mac?' Ronan questioned, settling himself between McCartney and Mum. 'What—like a coat?'

'No, Mac as in the first part of my name,' McCartney explained. 'Now I want to wander around the house and see which rooms would most benefit from a make-over. We have to choose the rooms which would be most televisually appealing.' He constructed a square with his forefingers and thumbs and peered into it with one eye.

'Wouldn't it be best to work on the room which most needs doing?' Dad suggested, as if it was most obvious thing in the world.

'Like my bedroom,' I volunteered.

'No, *my* bedroom,' Ronan added, quickly.

'No, not at all!' McCartney argued haughtily. 'The downstairs toilet might be the one room in the house which most needs doing but it wouldn't be at all practical to do that room.' He began to make notes about the lounge.

'Why not?' I asked. I was sitting on the floor in front of Dad's chair wondering why things had to be so complicated.

'First, there's the logistics of getting the camera crew into a small room . . .' McCartney explained.

'Then if any of us actually needs the loo,' Ronan said, smiling.

McCartney wasn't amused with that. 'And what we always have to remember is that we have to make it interesting for the television audience. They have to see a room that was awful at the beginning and is *totally* transformed.'

'So anything we say won't actually make much difference?' Mum asked, staring straight ahead.

'I'm afraid not,' McCartney answered honestly. 'Now I'd like some time alone to wander around the house and make my judgements about what we can do to make your home a more pleasant place.' He stood up quickly and began to pace around the lounge. Then he wandered out of the room and into the hall muttering away and scribbling furious notes as he went.

'Do you want to know something,' Mum said, looking miles away. 'It's all fallen into place.'

'What has?' Dad asked. He was watching McCartney Stephens and I know he was only half listening.

'This isn't about making us a better family at all,' Mum said. 'They're not going to turn us into a perfect family, are they?' She seemed a bit shocked at what she was saying.

'Well . . .' Dad began.

'No, they're not,' Mum insisted. 'They just want good television and we don't matter to them at all!'

Katie's Diary

Tuesday June 5th

Mac spent ages looking around the house yesterday deciding which rooms to choose. In the end he said we have to choose a room that's important for the kids and one for the grown-ups because we need to remember that grown-ups and kids are both watching this series. Mac said he wanted to transform my room because it was _so_ gross (I didn't think it was _that_ bad) and he said that would appeal to all the kids. He's also going to transform the kitchen — for the grown-ups.

I had to sit next to Mac on the floor in front of the cameras and tell him what I wanted him to do to my room. But it wasn't what I wanted because all I wanted was new wallpaper and a new quilt cover but he said it's not good television to say that. It will be over in two minutes of television time. I don't think so. It takes weeks for Mum and Dad to redecorate a room. That could take up a whole series. Mac thinks it would be far too boring just watching people wallpapering and painting.

It took five goes of me telling Mac what I wanted, (which was really what he wanted) in front of the camera and I kept getting it wrong, they said because I wasn't excited enough about it. I had to say that I wanted more storage space which I'm not bothered about and to say that I wanted really bright colours and a groovy place to bring my friends.

I would have liked a garden theme in my room with real plants and hedgehog-shaped bean bags and a hedgehog sort of cover on my bed. That would have been so brilliant. But Mac said it's not normal for girls of my age to want things like that.

How does he know? He knows nothing about girls of my age. He thinks we're all into make-up and pink walls and silly magazines all about boys but we're not. So I'm going to have these open cupboards in my room and they will be painted pink and yellow and turquoise. And when they start drilling and sawing and hammering, Mum will go mad. She won't be able to study.

At the end of the week, when the work is finished, I have to go into my room with a blindfold on and when Mac takes it off, I have to go, 'Wow! That's brilliant!' and pretend that I'm thrilled with my new cupboards and sparkly walls. See—Mac really knows buttons about girls.

Thursday June 7th

The noise is driving me mad. It's not just the hammering and the sawing. It's Mac whining on to the cameras and the camera crew working in Katie's room and all the charging up and down stairs. It's impossible to make myself a cup of tea in the kitchen because it's full of design consultants, directors, and carpenters and they look at me as if to say, 'Who are you? What are you doing in this kitchen?' I'm beginning to realize more and more that I'm very, very unimportant in the whole series. Nothing that I say or do is taken seriously and yet I can't explode in my own house because the cameras are there and next week the whole damn country would see me losing it.

I told Mac yesterday, then he started acting like a flaming therapist and said, 'If you want to shout and scream just get on with it.' Then when he thought I wasn't listening he said to Mauritia, 'That would be good television, wouldn't it?'

But I didn't lose it. I kept my dignity and went back to my studying, or trying to study, but it's so, so hard. I'm very down about everything. It isn't just the fact that I can't get my head around my revision. No, it's not just that, it's this family, my family. We're changing but not in the way we're supposed to be changing. We're not becoming a perfect family. We're not even becoming a better family. We're becoming strangers to one another and every noise of the hammer blow and every new piece of wood that's sawed makes me wonder why we ever volunteered for this.

For instance, last week we had Orlandia teaching Katie and Ronan how to cook, but somehow, Orlandia forgot to show them how to clear up after themselves. So I spent ages washing up every pot and pan we possess and wiping cooking stains off the wall. I'd like Orlandia to try doing that after a shift at the pork pie factory.

Then there's the garden. They're redoing it and putting lots of plants in so that we can entertain all our friends on summer evenings. But we're losing all our real friends because they don't want to be part of this dreadful spectacle and we seem to be acquiring awful new ones who long to be on the television.

We never seem to sit as a family and have a proper chat. Or even just enjoy one another's company. The cameras are always there, hovering over our shoulders like hawks ready to swoop on their prey — disagreements which make the drama they crave. Sometimes I forget that the cameras are there and I do lose it and then I feel awful for hours. I just shut myself away for fear of losing control again but it comes across as though I'm an immature mum in a huge sulk.

Then there are the letters. First they came from irate relations who asked us, 'Why are you doing this?' Then we had a few nice letters from 'fans', Mauritia called them. Now we're getting letters from cranks. I have to hide them from the children. They are so unkind.

The neighbours are up in arms about the disruption to the neighbourhood. Mr Thompson, the poodle man up at number 28, says we've lowered the tone of the whole area. 'You should have thought this through more carefully. Thought about the consequences.' Tell me about it! We've never had all that much to do with our neighbours—we were too busy. But we're certainly getting to know them now.

I'd love to say, 'Thanks for the experience, it was great. We're a much better family now. Can we leave it at that?'

But we can't. We've signed a legal contract with no opt-out clause. We're stuck with it.

Family Party

Dad's Diary

Sunday June 10th

It's very late on Sunday night. I'm sitting at the kitchen table writing my diary and Annie is on the other side of the table making notes for her English Literature exam, which is tomorrow. Every few minutes she stands and wanders around the room, muttering away as if she's forcing a point into her brain. Poor Annie, this is a big week for her with the exams but at least she has taken a few days' leave from the factory.

Mauritia called today and heaped more pressure on us, Annie in particular. She said we needed to talk about the next stage: Perfect Families Have Good Links With their Extended Family and Local Community. Katie and Ronan didn't have a clue what she was talking about. I tried to explain as best as I could. Mauritia interrupted me and said, with great excitement, 'Look, I realize that you're all getting a bit tired with the filming and everything, so I think the best way to deal with this part of the series is . . . well, what I think we need—is a party!'

Ronan and Katie, of course, were delighted. They love parties, always have, so when Mauritia started talking about a theme for the party they were in their element. It was wonderful to watch them being so enthusiastic about things but I could sense that Annie was very uncomfortable with the whole idea. She said, 'I think the last thing we need is a party, never mind a theme for the party.'

'Oh, don't be such a misery guts, Annie. A party would really perk you up!' Mauritia replied.

So Annie said, 'I'm not being a misery guts—I just want things to calm down a bit.'

Ronan offered to do the cooking which I thought was a really nice gesture. Katie said she'd do anything to help. 'A friend in need is a friend indeed, Mum,' she said.

Annie tried to explain but Mauritia kept interrupting her with bright, enthusiastic ideas. In the end, I decided to get a bit firm with Mauritia. 'You'll just have to listen for a few minutes, Mauritia,' I said. 'This is the wrong time for a party. I have just started a new job and this week is a critical one for Annie's exams. She has exams all day Monday, Tuesday, and Wednesday.'

Mauritia was quiet and serious for a few minutes then she said, 'Fine—we'll have a party on Friday and the only filming we'll do this week is at the party . . . or maybe just a little filming of the preparations.'

Ronan and Katie thought it was a great idea. 'It'll

really cheer us up,' Mauritia said. 'And I know it will be a huge success. We'll do all the organizing. All you have to worry about is your exams, OK?' The way she said it annoyed me because she made it sound as though Annie was just fretting about her . . . knitting or something.

She just doesn't understand.

Ronan's Diary

Tuesday June 12th

Changes. That's the theme for the party so we all have to be a bit different.

I am in charge of catering for the party. Not really. Mauritia's getting some mega-expensive caterers in but she said I could help out and choose the menus. The kitchen is all ready to roll so it should be a wicked, cool, cool party.

I rang Orlandia about the menu. She says don't do a barbecue because they are so twentieth century. But . . . it would be a shame not to use the brand new barbecue so . . . Orlandia says if you have to have a barbecue, you have to have twenty-first century marinades and sauces. What? Orlandia nearly flipped when

I asked her where you buy these marinades and sauces from. Actually she did flip, she went volcanic. She says, after all we went through the other week, you have to _make_ these sauces. Oops! Oh—and it has to be vegetarian. Meat's too unfashionable, Orlandia said. BSE and all that. Then Orlandia said I have to let the caterers do most of the work. What's the point of learning to cook if you get someone in to do it for you?

Anyway here's the menu that I worked out with the caterers:

Mixed raw vegetables with variety of dips, all home made.
Potato salad with grated parsnip dressing.
Spinach, broad bean, and beetroot salad.
Barbecued carrots with celery.
Barbecued peppers, chilli peppers, and baby corn.
Home made rosemary bread.
Prawn salad.
Green salad.
Ice cream and fresh fruit.
Pavlova.

It's a bit ambitious but it will be a wicked, wicked meal.

Must make a shopping list.

Need a lift to the supermarket.

Have to persuade Dad.

Dad sold the new kitchen to Mum—so funny. Dad gets commission for the new kitchen and we're not even paying for it! That is so clever!

Katie's Diary

Wednesday June 13th

The hedgehogs will never come to our garden now. Never. Julian Verde, the stupid, stupid garden designer, put up massive fences at the bottom of the garden where the wild animals used to get through. So now we're like a fortress to the foxes and the hedgehogs and even the neighbours' cats. (I don't mind about the cats because I'm fed up with their mess getting on to my trainers but I do mind about all the other creatures not being able to get into our garden.)

I have to sort out the tables and chairs for the garden. Mauritia is hiring a load because lots of people are coming to the party. All the neighbours have been invited. Some other people have been invited too but we don't know who they are because Mauritia wants it to be a surprise. We have got a party organizer helping us. She's called Taffeta. Honestly, aren't there any television people with normal names? Fancy calling a baby McCartney or Taffeta. Imagine picking it out of its cot and saying, 'Come on, McCartney, time for din-dins.' Or shouting down the street, 'Taffeta, you've got to come in now!' Everyone would crease up laughing. I suppose if you're called Taffeta, you don't play out on the street.

Mauritia says I have to pray for good weather. It's the middle of June so it should be fine. But if it rains . . .

Wednesday June 13th

No more exams until next week, thank goodness. It has been so hard concentrating these last few days. So much going on in the house but I've been that deep in my revision, I'm not even sure if Katie and Ronan have been going to school.

Yesterday, Taffeta, (what a name!) was wandering about the house worrying about the weather forecast for Friday. 'Rain spreading from the south, thundery showers, temperatures below the average expected for this time of year.' Mauritia suggested they check the Net for a more detailed picture.

'Then there's the cameras. We were banking on the weather being fine so that we could all spread out in the garden,' Mauritia mumbled. So I made a jokey suggestion which really turned things around. 'We could always get our tent out, that would provide a little shelter,' I said.

Taffeta was transformed. She called me a genius and clapped her hands together in delight. 'That's it! We'll hire a marquee!' she announced. I had only been joking about the tent. To be honest, I was a bit punch-drunk after all the revision.

Then, Taffeta decided that a marquee wasn't quite the same unless there was a band in the corner. So, there's a marquee going up in our garden on Friday.

What a fuss! I wonder what the neighbours will think of it.

On the evening of the party, the neighbours all arrived at the same time. It was quite funny, they were like an invading army. I felt like shouting, 'You may come in one at a time,' like the housekeeper does to Mary Poppins in the film.

They all trooped through, craning their necks as they did, to have a good look at our house. Then they marched into the marquee. Taffeta gave them a drink and they stood around asking about neighbourly things like . . . roses and strawberries and cabbages and new fences.

Ronan and the caterers put the food out on two trestle tables in the marquee. It didn't look like the sort of food you normally have at a party. Mr Thompson, the poodle man from number twenty-eight trotted over to the food and said, 'Now . . . what have we got here?'

'That's barbecued peppers and baby corn. I've just done them,' Ronan explained. He was really proud of himself. I wanted to say that I'd set out the chairs but I could tell that Mr Thompson wasn't really interested.

'I'll have a go at these, they look lovely. Why don't you try one, dear?' he said to his wife. He bit into the barbecued peppers and corn and began to chew. Then suddenly, he leaped about six feet into the air screaming, 'Water! Water! I'm on fire!'

Mrs Thompson wasn't as melodramatic, she simply called out, 'Oh, my God! It's so hot.'

I had done some fire prevention and first aid when I was in the Brownies so I knew exactly what to do if someone was on fire. I ran into the kitchen and grabbed an old towel. 'Move!' I screamed to Taffeta and ran back into the marquee. Mr Thompson was hopping about in great agitation. I couldn't see any flames but I wasn't taking any chances. The fire officer, who gave us the talk at the Brownies, said that your eyes sometimes deceive you in a fire. I shouted, 'Stand back everyone!' and then I threw the towel over Mr Thompson's head. (It was a particularly dirty and ragged old towel. The sort Dad uses for wiping stuff off the floor.)

'What the flaming hell are you doing?' Mr Thompson shouted in a muffled voice. He flung the towel off his head and across the marquee. 'Watch it!' Ronan panicked. He ran towards the food but it was too late. The filthy old towel landed on the buffet. The food was ruined.

'You're mad! Absolutely barking!' Mr Thompson yelled.

'There's no need to be like that, I have just saved your life!' I said, firmly.

Mrs Thompson, meanwhile, was twittering around like a demented butterfly. 'Why did you do that?' she asked.

'Mr Thompson said he was on fire,' I replied.

'It was my mouth, you silly, stupid girl!' he shouted.

What a scene! I felt very upset and Ronan was nearly crying. He kept going on about his food being ruined. 'It took me ages to get it ready. Days and days.' I wanted to point out that Ronan had been greatly helped by the caterers but I thought it was best to say nothing.

'I always thought this family was a bit strange,' Mr Thompson roared. 'Now I know for absolute certain that you're all doolally. All this demand for attention on the television!'

Taffeta placed her hand on Mr Thompson's arm and said, quietly, 'We are actually still . . . filming.' Mr Thompson stormed out of the marquee and almost dragged Mrs Thompson behind him.

Ronan was furious with me. 'Why did you do that, Katie?' he asked, looking desperate.

'Mr Thompson said he was on fire and a stitch in time saves nine,' I replied.

'It was just his mouth, you idiot!' Ronan exploded. 'You should have given him a drink of water . . .'

'I'm not a mind reader, Ronan!' I snapped. 'I didn't know it was just his mouth. Anyway, you shouldn't have used those things, those hot peppers.'

As I turned round, away from Ronan, I noticed that the cameras were still working—one on me and Ronan, one on the neighbours who were as far away from us as possible. As though we had a highly contagious disease. Like the plague.

I felt awful.

Ronan's Diary

Friday June 15th

This is what I can't stand about neighbours. They pretend to be nice, all the time. Hello, Ronan, you're getting a big lad, aren't you growing up quickly. Hello, you young shaver, and all that. But deep down all they want is to have a good look in your house just to know that they're much better than you.

All our neighbours are like that. They always just say hello but now they want to be great friends with all of us just 'cause we're on the telly. Well, I don't want to be friends with any of them, especially Mr Poodle Man Thompson. I didn't know chilli peppers were hot. Nobody told me and it didn't say in the recipe. It said it was an exciting taste.

Katie shouldn't have thrown the towel. Sometimes she thinks it's her job to save the world and all the hedgehogs in it. It isn't. Why *can't somebody tell her that? And tell her to stop those stupid sayings. I was so, so gutted when the food was ruined. But that wasn't the worst bit. Taffeta rang up Burger-to-Go on Main Street and ordered loads of burgers and sausages and pizzas. Junk! Then everyone tucked into it. I just sat at the side of the tent watching our greedy neighbours eating poisonous junk food and listening to a pathetic band.*

What a party. What a disaster!

Dad overslept the morning after the party. I woke him to remind him that he was on an early shift but he said he couldn't face going to work. I don't know why. They haven't shown our party on the telly yet. Mum says she's emigrating when they do. She's gone to the library in town while they pack away the big tent.

It was very strange at the party after Mr Poodle stormed off. Everything was quiet for a bit and then the doorbell rang. Taffeta answered it and came back in with this man we had never seen before. Dad looked at him like he knew him from somewhere. Taffeta clapped her hands as if it was her birthday and she'd got a new Barbie. 'Michael,' she said, with a great flourish, 'this is your long-lost brother, Brian!'

Dad didn't smile as if he was overjoyed to see Brian or anything. He looked at Brian and the lady standing next to him. Uncle Brian said, 'This is my partner, Sunshine.'

'Michael, isn't it lovely to see your brother after all these years?' Taffeta trilled.

'Of course it is,' Dad replied but he didn't smile or look as if he meant it.

Brian spoke like an Australian and Sunshine sort of twirled around the party like a film star. Dad didn't talk much to Brian except to ask him where he was staying and Brian said, 'Here.' Dad disappeared for ages and came back with Mum who'd been sitting inside the house talking to Mrs Stelanicki, our next door neighbour.

'Any chance you two could find a quiet corner and reminisce about the old days?' Taffeta asked, charmingly.

'I'd rather not,' Dad said, flatly. 'It's nice to see Brian and find out about his life in Australia but I'm definitely not getting into any talking about the old days . . . and I'm sorry, but we don't have enough space to let you stay here, at the moment, Brian.' (For some reason, we don't hear much about Uncle Brian because he had a big fall out with Dad a long time ago and then Uncle Brian went to Australia.)

'Aren't you a funny family?' Isla said after Uncle Brian appeared at the party. (All of Isla's family had been invited because they're our neighbours but only Isla decided to come.) 'My mum says that you've been chosen for this series because you're a bit odd.'

'And I suppose your family's already perfect, Isla,' I snapped. What a cheek!

'Well, actually, that's why we didn't get chosen,' Isla said, smugly.

Isla made me feel really, really annoyed. I felt very sad about lots of things, not just Isla—throwing the towel, the hedgehogs . . . well, everything. Dad was fed up about Uncle Brian and Ronan wasn't speaking to me.

'I think I'm coming down with something,' Mum said. 'I feel like I want to go to bed for a few months.'

What a mess.

Saturday June 16th

Yesterday was the day when I really regretted doing this. Not for myself but for Annie mostly, and the children. The party was an unbelievable failure. We managed, somehow, to upset the neighbours and fall out with one another. In the midst of all that, my brother arrived. I've never got on with Brian. He was my big brother and he was a bully. It was the best day of my life when he went away.

You see, it was his fault that the ice cream company collapsed. It had been going strong since 1935 and then Brian took it over and within two years it failed. My poor dad was devastated. Brian had spent everything and then he disappeared. A few years later he turned up in Australia.

I didn't want the children to find out about Brian. I wanted it to be a secret, always in the past.

Now the whole country knows.

HEARTLANDS TELEVISION
Gable Oak • Nottingham

Saturday June 17th

Dear Michael, Annie, Ronan, and Katie,

I think it's safe to say that we're all a bit weary of the intensive changes and the filming. So . . . what about we all go away on holiday for a few days? All expenses paid, of course!

We'll invite Clement de Conservatoire, World Famous Therapist, along. He'll advise about family dynamics but I think it will be great to get completely away from home for this.

Shall we go somewhere . . . not too far, yet with good hotels, nice views, and lovely food. We want to show our viewers that 'Perfect Families get on well with one another and enjoy spending time together.'

The reviews and letters continue to pour in. All very favourable. Michael's reunion with Brian has touched many hearts.

Have a wonderful holiday,

regards,

Mauritia

Monday June 19th

Mauritia clicks her fingers, stamps her feet, and we're all supposed to jump. We're supposed to be going on holiday. The cameras were rolling early, waiting for Mauritia's note to arrive. Michael read it and passed it to me. He didn't say anything, not good television. But I said something, oh yes, I said something. My final exam is on Wednesday. All my hard work for two years will be wasted because Mauritia wants us to go on holiday.

But it's not just me—I don't like Katie and Ronan missing school during term time. I want them to do well at school. And I don't want Michael to miss time from his new job. I know it's a bit boring to say this but we can't afford it. If they're trying to make us into the perfect family, they're making a bit of a mess of it.

Mauritia arrived at midday, full of apologies, five minutes before I was due to leave the house for an exam. 'So sorry,' she said. 'My researchers have really let me down on this one. Didn't know you had exams this week. Really should have been more sensitive, but sometimes when you're improving something it gets worse before it gets better, blah, blah, blah . . . '

I was desperate to get out of the house so I reached a compromise with Mauritia. So – this is what's going to happen: we're leaving straight after school on Wednesday so Ronan and Katie will only miss two days' school. Michael will have to take some holiday. Meanwhile, the cameras will film our preparation. They're not filming me because I'm going to get my head down. Back to my revision.

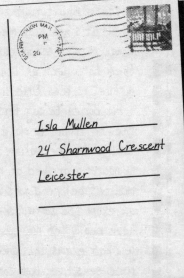

Dear Isla and Krishna,
Hope you're OK. It's brilliant not being at school. We are staying in a superb hotel in Scarborough. I have got a room to myself and I can watch TV whenever I want to. Ronan has been running on the beach in the morning and Mum and Dad are just enjoying the rest and the scrummy food. Yum! I have taken loads of brilliant photos especially at the sea-life centre. It's got a lovely atmosphere inside it. We have been on the funfair every day. Mauritia has given us loads of money to spend.
See you on Monday,
        lots of love, Katie

Isla Mullen
24 Sharnwood Crescent
Leicester

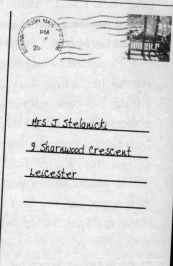

Dear Mrs Stelanicki,   22nd June
Thanks for checking the house for us while
we're away. It is so good of you. I'll have to
buy you a huge stick of seaside rock! We are
staying at the North Atlantic Marina Hotel
and it is absolutely gorgeous. The food is
wonderful, too. Just exactly what I needed
after my final exam.
But ... it's not all fun. Every morning we
have group and individual meetings with this
family therapist. It can be a bit painful.
Still, we always have lunch to look forward to!
The sun has been shining non-stop and we're
all beginning to unwind. The only thing is, the
cameras are still around.
Still, nothing's perfect.
See you soon,
Annie and family

Mrs J Stelanicki

9 Sharnwood Crescent

Leicester

We left for Scarborough on the Wednesday afternoon, full
of hope and excitement. It was hot and sunny and the
beach was golden, the sea really blue. The food was
wonderful. Everything was just right, until . . . well, we all
had to have a meeting with Clement, who's a world-
famous family therapist. He's the man who's supposed to
be helping us get on with one another.

It was my turn to talk to Clement first. He was sitting in
a small hotel room with the cameras at one end. For some
reason, I felt very nervous. Clement asked me about my
interests. I told him that I liked nature and trying to attract
wild animals into the garden. I felt quite strange when he

asked me why I liked doing this. I stared at him for ages and then I said, 'Mum and Dad won't let me keep a real pet of my own and I've read about hedgehogs so I'm trying to rescue one and keep it as a pet.'

He seemed to be pleased with my responses so he asked me to get Mum and Dad from the lounge. They were sitting on two sofas, reading the papers and drinking coffee. They both looked very relaxed and content, the best they'd been for ages.

'Finished, Katie?' Dad asked, looking up.

'He wants to see you and Mum with me, now,' I said. Mum stroked my hair and smiled at me like she hadn't done for ages, as we walked to the room. The break was doing her good.

As soon as we were in the room, the cameras started filming again and Clement asked, 'What do you think of your daughter?'

'What a daft question!' Mum remarked, smiling at Clement.

'Is it?' Clement's eyebrows rose as he spoke.

'Well, of course it is,' Mum said quickly.

'We think she's wonderful, of course,' Dad said. I didn't feel wonderful. I was sitting on the very edge of my seat and I could feel the tension building up. The atmosphere in the room had changed so quickly.

'You think she's wonderful but you won't allow her to have a pet?' Clement stated.

'No,' Mum agreed.

'Whyever not?' he questioned. 'It's the most natural thing in the world for a child to have a pet of their own but your deprived daughter has to encourage wild animals to come into her garden so that she can develop her caring instincts. Why won't you buy her a pet?'

I wanted to interrupt him because he was turning things around and making me look as though I was talking behind Mum's and Dad's backs. But my throat was all dry.

'She's not old enough to look after one,' Mum replied, calmly. 'And by the way, she's *not* deprived.'

'You know what happens, Clement,' Dad said, trying to lighten the situation. 'They get the pet, say a hamster or a guinea pig, they love it and care for it for a few weeks but after that they get fed up with it. *Then* Mum and Dad have to take care of it.'

'So . . . what's the problem?' Clement questioned. 'It's the same for all parents.'

'We just don't have the time at the moment,' Mum sighed. Which was true, I understood that.

'So you don't have any time for your children!' Clement said.

'No, for any pets,' Mum said quickly. 'Besides, I didn't think Katie was all that bothered about a pet, are you, Katie?'

'Katie?' Clement swivelled around to face me.

'I don't know,' I said, uncomfortably.

'What do you mean, Katie?' Mum asked, impatiently. Dad touched Mum's arm as if to quieten her.

'Well, I just wanted the hedgehogs,' I began.

'Go on, Katie,' Clement encouraged.

'I don't know really,' I said, hesitantly. 'I'm not sure what I want any more.'

'Well, thank you, Clement!' Mum snapped. 'You're certainly helping our family get on with one another. I *don't* think!'

And the cameras were still filming.

Katie's Diary

Sunday June 27th

It wasn't my fault. I didn't say ANYTHING about wanting a pet. He just asked me about my interests and then it all sort of exploded. They started arguing about pets. He was horrible to my mum and dad. Horrible.

But they didn't fight with him. They were fighting with one another. Dad says, I always wanted to buy Katie a guinea pig but you wouldn't let me. Mum says, they're too much bother, then Clement says, you're lazy, Annie. And all the time they're filming my mum and dad. I'm trying to make this family better, Clement says, but you won't change at all. Katie needs a pet, he kept saying, she needs to believe in herself. She needs more attention.

What about Ronan? Dad says. Clement says, Ronan's too arrogant and he gets his own way too much. Katie has to fit in around everyone else. I never said it. HE DID.

And it's true. I'm fed up with fitting in with everyone else. (Even though it makes everyone argue when I don't) I'm fed up with the filming. I don't want to be part of a perfect family any more— I've had enough of it.

Family Illness

Ronan's Diary

Tuesday June 29th
Clement is a _head case_. He's like a chemical
you put into liquid to make it effervesce only
he's made the liquid explode and hit the walls.

Scarborough was brilliant for about three
days then Clement ruined it. Everyone at my
running club thinks my family are fighting dogs.
We're not like that, really. They've cut out all
the good bits. I've seen them doing it, I've
heard them discussing it. 'For good television,'
they say, 'you have to edit!'

Well, they've edited our smiles and all the
nice times we had together in Scarborough
right out of the picture. Makes me sick.

Mum's Diary

Tuesday June 29th

We're not famous. We're infamous. The latest headline reads: 'How TV's Perfect Family Neglected Daughter.'

Great.

Millions of people now know I'm a useless mother.

Dad's Diary

Wednesday June 30th

Scarborough was full of great promise at the beginning of the week—lovely sunshine, beautiful beach, excellent hotel, exceptional food. Mauritia said it was going to be a break away from everyone and everything. But it was a disaster, a complete disaster.

Annie hasn't spoken to me since we returned home. Work has been dreadful, I haven't sold a single kitchen and Ronan and Katie seem to be bickering all the time.

What are we going to do? We can't go on like this.

What _are_ we going to do?

HEARTLANDS TELEVISION
Gable Oak • Nottingham

Thursday July 1st

Dear Michael, Annie, Ronan, and Katie,
How does it feel to be so famous and such stars? I'm enclosing a review of this week's programme from the local paper. It's true what they say: you are such a courageous family. Hope you're all looking forward to the final studio session next week where we'll meet representatives from the Milton Keynes Research Institute. This is a surprise session so . . . we hope it will be a good one.

Transport will be arranged for you so that you'll arrive at the studio in style and on time.

See you soon,

Mauritia

Bravehearted family

There aren't many families who would put themselves through torture. But the Rossi family have surpassed themselves this week with their disastrous holiday in Scarborough. What a family! What a series! Still one more episode of this epic drama to go.

Reality television at its very best. ∎

Thursday July 1st

Soon as we arrived back from Scarborough Mum went straight to bed and she hasn't got up since. Dad had to go back to work on Monday so me and Ronan have been doing everything. Every time I go up to see Mum she's asleep or crying and she won't eat anything. When we go to the studio in Nottingham, all the camera stuff is going to be taken out of the house so the filming has finished.

Mum thinks we made a big mistake doing this. She says we've lost all our friends and everybody thinks we're just an odd family. I haven't lost my friends but Isla and Krishna are a bit different with me and ... well, I used to be really close to Krishna and now they're very close and I'm sort of the odd one out.

I still don't know why everyone wants to be famous because it's the most horrible thing ever. People don't just stare at you on the street and point at you. They walk over and turn you around so that their friends can look at you. They think that just because you've been on their

telly that they sort of own you. They
think they can do anything they like with
you and that's the worst, worst bit. And
Isla says they'll always be like that to
you because they'll always remember you
as the hedgehog girl, who wanted her
own pet who was once on the telly. She
says they'll never forget me.

Ronan's Diary

Monday July 5th

There's an absolutely wicked stretch limousine
outside our house waiting to take us to the
studio in Nottingham. I can't wait to jump in and
switch on the telly and have a drink of ice cool
Coke and wave at all the neighbours who are
gazing out and wishing it was them doing it in
luxury. But I don't think we'll be going anywhere.

The thing is, Mum absolutely refuses to get
up. She says she's had enough of everything and
she doesn't want to get up again, ever.

Mrs Stelanicki has made the driver a cup of
tea and he's sitting in her front garden

drinking and eating some of Mrs Stelanicki's
cake. Dad has tried to get Mum up and so has
Katie. Even Mrs Stelanicki came up and
pleaded with Mum. She told Dad to ring the
doctor. The doctor won't come. He said Dad's
got to take Mum up to the surgery but she
won't get out of bed. Dad got really angry with
the doctor and he said, 'What if she was
dying?' but the doctor just said, 'Well is she?
Dying?' Then Dad's been on the phone to
Mauritia and Mauritia's been trying to
persuade Mum to get in the stretch limo and
just go to Nottingham and get it all over with.
But she won't.

   Looks like we won't get a ride in it.

Tuesday July 6th

I had no choice. I had to go. Mauritia arrived with a doctor and a lawyer. The doctor said I was totally exhausted. He gave me some tablets to keep me going over the next few days. Mauritia's lawyer was a rottweiler 'You signed a contract,' he reminded me, 'for the whole series!'

'I can't go on,' I said.

'You have no choice,' he snarled. 'If you don't go, Heartlands Television will sue you for breach of contract and you could lose everything.'

'We don't have anything to lose,' I told him.

'You could lose your home,' he warned.

'But I thought this was all about making better families,' I said.

'It's about good television,' he growled.

I had no choice. I had to go.

Part Three

Change the Family

Every Picture Tells a Story

Well it does, doesn't it. Everyone who looked at us agreed that we were a changed family. All the publicity photographs revealed a different family. They didn't show how ill Mum was or anything like that. When we arrived at the studio, Mum could hardly walk but nobody asked how she felt. They were only bothered with getting us on to the studio floor for the live broadcast. The last programme in the series.

There we were, sitting on the studio sofa, waiting for the opening credits to finish. The audience began to clap. As soon as the applause subsided, Marianna declared, 'Meet the Perfect Family,' and the cameras zoomed in on Mum, Dad, Ronan, and me. More applause. We smiled, like professional celebrities, then we waved at the audience and at the cameras. I thought we were like an optical illusion—we *looked* happy.

Marianna reminded the cameras of our appearance eight weeks ago, before the transformation began. A photograph of the family sitting on that same studio sofa was held up for all to see. 'Look at the wonderful change in the appearance of this lovely family,' Marianna enthused. 'What a difference!'

'Yes,' Pascal agreed. 'I'm especially delighted with Mum.' He wrapped his arm around Mum's shoulders. 'Look how much weight she has lost. Doesn't she look wonderful? I'm so glad she decided to go to the gym.'

Mum smiled and tossed back her freshly cut hair. The fact that she had eaten almost nothing in the last few days wasn't mentioned.

'Do you feel much happier, Annie, now that you're so young and fit looking?' Marianna questioned.

'Definitely,' Mum replied. She had been advised to give short, simple responses, not to give too much away.

'And Michael, your hair looks *really* different . . . what have you done to it?' Marianna asked.

'Now there's a story, Marianna,' Dad said. Marianna giggled like a little girl before Dad continued. 'I didn't go for a hair transplant. I couldn't possibly go through all that pain. I took Annie's advice and had my hair closely cropped. Apparently, it's very fashionable,' Dad said, his arms slightly outstretched.

'I'll say it is,' Marianna agreed. '*You* look wonderful, too!' The audience applauded Dad's hair and then Marianna said, 'Michael and Annie, you must be very proud of your two wonderful children. They have taken to all this with such confidence and aplomb. Ronan, you're almost like a professional.'

'It's been absolutely wicked,' Ronan said. 'I think I'd like to be on the television when I grow up.' Marianna laughed at that.

'What about you, Katie? How do you feel now we're almost at the end of this series?' Marianna asked.

'I think I'll miss everyone,' I said. 'We've had some great fun but it's been hard at times.' (That's what I'd been told to say.)

'Tell me something, Katie, between you and me—have those hedgehogs come into your garden yet?'

'No . . . but I'm still trying,' I replied.

Marianna smiled at what I said and then she swivelled around to face another camera. 'Now we're going to welcome back the brains behind this whole project—the man who told us what perfect families are all about. Ladies and gentlemen, I'd like to welcome Dr Paul Martin from the Milton Keynes Institute for the Family.' After a brief pause for applause, Marianna continued. 'Dr Paul— what do you think makes the perfect family?'

'Well, Marianna, it's all those things we've talked about over the last few weeks plus one very important one . . .'

'Would you like to tell us what that is?' Marianna interrupted.

'I must say, first of all, that what everyone needs to understand is that this has been a fantastic scientific experiment.'

'What?' Mum asked quietly. Dad gently touched her arm.

'Don't get me wrong,' Dr Paul corrected himself. 'As well as being wonderfully entertaining television, it has also been brilliant research for family experts like myself.'

Something about the way Dr Paul was speaking made me feel really uneasy. It was as though he didn't realize we were there. He didn't look at us. He looked over our heads at Marianna as though we were a meaningless rabble who were simply cluttering up the studio.

'I would agree with you there,' Marianna interrupted.

'It has been a fantastic experience for all of us,' Dr Paul continued. 'For many it has been the highlight of the summer—watching what the Rossis are getting up to each week . . .'

That was the moment when I wanted to escape from the studio because they were making me feel as though we were a family of chimpanzees in the primate house at Twycross Zoo. I could hear what they were saying but their voices began to sound fuzzy.

'So . . . the last item on the list, about the perfect family is . . . Well, there is no such thing as a *perfect* family.'

'That's fascinating, Dr Paul,' Marianna said. What was fascinating about that? I felt so angry and I could feel Mum and Dad becoming restless.

But Dr Paul was really wound up and there seemed to be no stopping him. 'In a way it has been like a home improvement programme. You know, where the woodwork and the walls are stripped and thoroughly sanded down before the team make their creative mark on a room. That's where the Rossis are today and it's very important for them to remember that, of course, being a perfect family hasn't really got anything to do with hairstyles or clothes or food. It's about loving each other and supporting each other.'

I wanted to scream at the top of my voice, 'What? After all we've been through, you're telling us there's no such thing as a perfect family.' But I couldn't, I wasn't allowed to. The contract. We were warned before we came on. 'It will be controversial, it will be hard and you will want to argue about things. But DON'T.'

'So, there is no such thing as the perfect family,' Marianna announced. 'Annie, Michael, Ronan, and Katie: what do you feel about that?'

For one awkward moment there was complete silence, (not good television,) as we digested Dr Paul's words. Then Mum leaned her head back against the studio sofa as if she was opting out.

'I'll tell you what I feel,' Dad began. 'Betrayed! I feel betrayed!' Marianna nodded her head like a wise owl listening to a noisy chick. Behind the cameras I could see Mauritia smiling but the other researchers were a bit fidgety.

'I feel like we've been tricked, really,' Mum said, quietly, without raising her head.

141

'What makes you say that, Annie?' Marianna questioned.

There was another silent pause as Mum sat upright, cleared her throat, and smoothed out her skirt. 'We're been jumping through hoops and having our lives turned upside down for weeks and weeks to make ourselves into the perfect family and now *you*,' Mum shouted, pointing at Dr Paul, '. . . *you* tell us that there is *no such thing* as the perfect family!'

'In a sense, that's true,' Dr Paul said, defensively. 'Every family is very different and imperfect in their own little way.'

'Nobody's perfect,' I said. Ronan glared at me.

'Very true,' Dr Paul agreed. 'And what we all need is to work hard to make our families *happy*.'

'Well, we're not happy any more,' Mum said, confidently.

Marianna worked hard to recover the situation. 'But at least you're famous now. Everyone in the country knows you . . .'

'What is so good about being famous?' Mum asked.

'It's horrible being famous!' I added. I was like Dad, I felt betrayed, too. What did Marianna think was good about being famous?

'Anyway, we're not famous!' Mum snapped. 'We're infamous—a laughing stock. Something for the nation to laugh at in summer. Cheaper than making a new situation comedy!'

'You're right, Annie,' Dad agreed. 'We even wrote our own script.'

'And you haven't made our family any better,' Ronan argued. 'You haven't fixed the microwave or the toaster and I still have to walk to training!'

'What you, as a family, have to remember is that you volunteered for this,' Dr Paul stated, ignoring Ronan's comments. 'Nobody *made* you do it. You were very willing.'

Marianna quickly swivelled around to face yet another camera as the floor director indicated that we should be quiet. 'So . . . the main thing is—what lessons have the Rossi family learned from this experience?' she questioned.

'I know what I've learned,' I said. 'It isn't cool to be famous. It's awful. Horrible!'

'I hear what you're saying, Katie—fame has it's price,' Marianna said, nodding her head sympathetically.

'What's that supposed to mean?' Mum questioned. 'You haven't a clue what we're talking about. You live in a beautiful country house, with no demanding kids, surrounded by acres of peaceful countryside. You never have to worry about money or exam results. How could you possibly know what it's like for us?'

'Calm down, love,' Dad advised.

'No! I won't calm down!' Mum snapped. 'We're still living in the same poxy house which has been almost *ruined* by your "home improvers". We're still struggling to make ends meet; we still have a huge overdraft; still worrying about the future; all our friends have deserted us, and we're bombarded with letters from nutters! We're not a perfect family, nor will we *ever* be. We're a stupid, foolish family and I wish we had never seen that advertisement in the paper!'

'So do I,' I agreed. And I meant it. That was one of the worst mistakes I ever made, ringing up the television company, and at that moment I really, really regretted it.

'Me too,' Ronan muttered.

'Yes,' Dad nodded.

'So *don't*,' Mum stood up and pointed at Marianna, shouting, '*don't* you dare tell me that fame has its price. Fame has ruined,' Mum screeched, '. . . *ruined* our fami—' Mum's legs crumpled underneath her as she slumped to the floor. My heart stopped.

'Mum!' I called. She didn't answer. I felt faint.

The cameras swivelled away from us. Marianna looked only slightly concerned, as she said, 'That's all from us. We'll see you again in the autumn with a brand-new make-over programme. Until then, goodbye!'

'I think we need an ambulance!' Dr Paul cried.

Dad cradled Mum. Ronan and I stroked her hands. 'I'm so, so sorry,' Dad said, tearfully. 'You didn't want any of this.'

HEARTLANDS TELEVISION
Gable Oak • Nottingham

Monday July 12th

Dear Michael, Annie, Ronan, and Katie,
Congratulations! Superb end to a fantastic
series. Have you read the reviews? You were
all so brilliant. We love you.

I'm off to Thailand for three weeks.
Desperately need a break.

Be in touch when I return,

Mauritia

Wednesday July 14th
Mum had to go to hospital. The doctor said she was exhausted and he told her to start eating again. Everyone's talking about Mum collapsing in the studio. We've even been on the news!

Yesterday at school was horrible.
Another note:

Now that your mum's ill
we've had our fill
of your poxy pathetic family.

I wasn't going to show it to Mum and Dad but we've had loads of letters from people. Nasty letters. And then there were cameras outside on the street. Different cameras, not Mauritia's. They filmed us coming and going. There's crowds of nosy parkers, too, coming round to point at our house and say, 'That's where they live.'

The neighbours are all angry because the street's clogged up. Even Mrs Stelanicki is angry and she was our best friend. Mum got her money from the pork pie factory but they sacked her after Monday's programme.

Mum says she wants to disappear, become invisible for a few weeks. Then they'll forget about us. Dad says that's a good idea. Let's disappear. Let's just go where nobody can see us.

So we did.

Six months later, things *have* settled down, as you can see from this cutting. It was in one of the weekend magazines.

January 16th

PERFECT FAMILY RETURNS

It sounded like a dream come true for Annie and Michael Rossi and their children, Ronan and Katie. Their chance to improve their lives and become the perfect family. But it didn't work out that way.

Six months on, the Rossi family reflect on their life since the dramatic climax to the series. 'We had to get away,' Annie reveals. 'We were at the centre of a media frenzy so we had to just leave, take a break.'

The Rossi family headed for the small town of Mackay in Queensland, Australia, where Michael's brother owns an ice cream parlour. 'The one good thing that has happened,' Michael says, in a voice tinged with emotion, 'is that Brian and I were reconciled and that's something I thought would never happen.'

'We had a wonderful holiday,' Annie recalls. 'Brian and Sunshine were so kind and warm towards us.'

Now, back in Britain, the Rossi family are philosophical about their brush with fame. 'It was a laugh at first,' Ronan says, 'But then it turned sort of nasty.'

'School was hell,' Katie remembers.

The Rossi family have moved on. They sold their house and bought another one a few streets away. Annie is in the first year of her degree at a local university; Michael is working as a classroom assistant with a penchant for telling great stories; and Ronan and Katie? Well, they are just getting on with their lives. Would they do it again? 'Never!' they reply with one voice. 'It almost ruined us.'

■

It's almost a year since that fateful day when we saw the advertisement in the paper, since we started out on our epic adventure. Me and Dad and Ronan thought it would be a good thing but Mum didn't. Why didn't we listen to her? Why didn't we realize from the very beginning that we couldn't be a perfect family? Why did we want to be on the television and the fame that went with it? I'm still not sure.

These days it seems as though everybody wants to be famous. Really, really famous. But when you're famous, people want to know everything about you; they want to look at every single bit of your life with a magnifying glass. Then they laugh at the bad bits and sneer at the things you want to keep hidden. That's what is so horrible about being on the television. You just can't hide. Anywhere.

We're sort of hiding now. There's no more cameras. Nobody knows where we live any more. We've moved—to a smaller house but it's much nicer. Dad loves his new job and Mum's concentrating on her degree. There's no more early shifts in the pork pie factory.

Mum says when things have settled down and people have forgotten about us, Krishna can come for tea. She's still my friend but it's not like it used to be and that makes me sad. I found out that Isla and Conor wrote those horrible notes. Now that we've moved, I don't have to walk home with Isla any more so there's no reason for us to be friends.

When Krishna comes for tea I can show her our garden. It backs on to an old railway line so there's lots of wildlife about. Real proper wildlife, not just squirrels.

When we were in Australia, Sunshine told me lots about hedgehogs. She said they like a peaceful garden where nobody can notice them. They don't like a lot of attention. (That meant I had to stop checking for them every morning.) Mum helped me to put some old wood next to the hedge and, after the rain, I collected lots of slugs from the neighbours and put them near the pile of wood. And guess what? The hedgehog has arrived!

Everything comes to she who waits. Even hedgehogs.